# TEN TOMBSTONES TO TEXAS

*Other books in this series available from New English Library:*

No 1 EDGE: THE LONER
No 2 EDGE: TEN THOUSAND DOLLARS AMERICAN
No 3 EDGE: APACHE DEATH
No 4 EDGE: KILLER'S BREED
No 5 EDGE: BLOOD ON SILVER
No 6 EDGE: THE BLUE, THE GREY AND THE RED
No 7 EDGE: CALIFORNIA KILLING
No 8 EDGE: SEVEN OUT OF HELL
No 9 EDGE: BLOODY SUMMER
No 10 EDGE: VENGEANCE IS BLACK
No 11 EDGE: SIOUX UPRISING
No 12 EDGE: THE BIGGEST BOUNTY
No 13 EDGE: A TOWN CALLED HATE
No 14 EDGE: THE BIG GOLD
No 15 EDGE: BLOOD RUN
No 16 EDGE: THE FINAL SHOT
No 17 EDGE: VENGEANCE VALLEY

# Edge: Ten Tombstones to Texas

GEORGE G. GILMAN

NEW ENGLISH LIBRARY
TIMES MIRROR

for
F.B.
who co-operated in selling a
book or two!

A New English Library Original Publication


*

FIRST NEL PAPERBACK EDITION FEBRUARY 1976

*



*NEL Books are published by*
*New English Library Limited from Barnard's Inn, Holborn, London, E.C.1.*
*Made and printed in Great Britain by Hunt Barnard Printing Ltd., Aylesbury, Bucks.*

45002660 4

## Chapter One

A HALF-MOON hung low and bright in the cloudless sky to spread deep shadows among the ridges and gorges of the Sierra Nevada range. But Muriel and Mathilda Tree had long ago learned it was foolish to be afraid of the dark. Thus, it was something less tenuous than rock shade and pools of darkness among the rugged terrain of the high country that caused the two women to remain alert to danger as they made camp.

The site they had chosen was a good one: on a broad shelf of level ground at the base of a towering cliff. The high rock wall protected them to the south. Looking north, they could see the entire length of a wide valley through which they had approached this place. There was the cover of broken ground down there and one man might have been able to get close if he was careful. But not a whole bunch of men: there were just too many areas of moon-bright open ground between the dark dips and the scattered outcrops of rock. To the east and the west there was enough cover to conceal a small army until it was within two hundred feet of the campsite. But, in addition to learning how to pick the best places to rest up each night, the women had also adjusted to the fact that they could never expect perfection. In the wide and wild country of the western United States, travellers had to take what the terrain offered and adapt to it. The land was a niggardly giver and those who accepted its terms had to compromise.

This and much else had not been easily learned, for the school was that of experience, gained as the women made the gruelling journey south from the now distant border of the United States with the Dominion of Canada.

'You agree this is a good place to stop for the night, Aunt Matty?' the younger woman asked after she had made a thorough survey from the seat of the covered wagon.

'I think it's a fine place, my dear,' Mathilda Tree answered, stifling a yawn and raising herself a little off the seat to massage her rump. 'And I think it's certainly time that we called a halt.'

'If you ate more, like I'm always telling you, this rig wouldn't feel so hard to you, Aunt Matty,' Muriel said with a smile as she coiled the reins around the brake lever and expertly swung down to the ground.

The older woman was slower in her movements, grimacing as stiff joints were forced into painful action. 'And like I'm always telling you, when a girl has got a homely face and a fine body, she'd be a fool not to take care of her figure.'

Muriel, with her back to her aunt, smiled again as she made a reappraisal of the approaches to the campsite. At sixty-two, Aunt Matty was by no stretch of the imagination a girl. But, by rigorous attention to what she ate, she did have a figure which many girls would envy. And she carried it better than most girls less than half her age. Mathilda Tree was a slender five feet nine inches tall and she always stood and moved at her full height, often having to hide the pain she experienced from the rheumatics that were apt to bother her. Unfortunately, her features were no match for the well preserved lines of her body. In a framework of wiry dyed blonde hair, her face was little short of ugly. Her forehead was too low, her brown eyes were too small and too far apart; her nose was too big and her mouth was too wide, the lips too thin. In addition, her skin was lined and toughened by the passage of hard-lived years and she had a cluster of hair-sprouting moles on the side of her jaw. Once during her younger days before her complexion deteriorated, she had tried to improve her facial looks with paint and powder. But no longer. The men who she constantly sought to attract had to accept her in the way nature had fashioned her. Five of them had done so to the ultimate extent of marrying her.

'My turn for the feeding, Mu?' Aunt Matty called meekly from the other side of the wagon.

Muriel completed her second, searching surveillance of the surrounding terrain and knew she was as satisfied as she was ever going to be that they were alone in this piece of country.

'You know very well it is,' she replied with a sigh. 'And you ought to know by know that he won't hurt you.'

'That's something I'm never going to be sure about, my dear,' Aunt Matty muttered sourly. 'He's got the evil eye and he hates me, I know.'

The object of the woman's apprehension was a pure white bull that was hitched to the tail-gate of the wagon. He was an enormous beast weighing more than three and a half thousand pounds with small, pricked ears and curved horns that were only slightly larger. He stood motionless and docile behind the parked wagon and only his dark, flat, unblinking eyes moved as the woman appeared.

'Steady, feller,' Aunt Matty soothed as she gingerly reached out to release the peg and lower the tail-gate. 'Nice bull. Time for grub. Good old Aunt Matty's going to feed you.'

The bull flared his nostrils and swished his tail. He maintained his unblinking stare. There was a set of steps hung at the side of the wagon and the woman used these to climb up into the back. Three-quarters of the freight space was thickly packed with animal fodder and it was necessary to unfasten the wire of a new bale. While she did this, Aunt Matty did not take her fearful eyes off the placid bull. For his part, the animal did not move. She tore at the fodder with her long-nailed fingers and scattered almost half the bale on the hard-packed dirt behind the wagon. Then, with an easy strength, she climbed down the steps carrying the remains of the bale. She backed away from the bull, who lowered his massive head and began to feed.

'You're an evil-minded hunk of beefsteak on legs, that's what you are!' the woman taunted softly from a safe distance.

'Still in one piece, Aunt Matty?' Muriel called lightly.

'He's saving himself,' the older woman answered as she returned to the front of the wagon. She bent her head to wipe her brow free of the sweat of fear on her coat sleeve. 'For the time when I'm not looking at him and he can surprise me. He hates me, I tell you.'

She had no fear of horses and her actions as she unhitched the four stallions comprising the team were deft and confident. But she continued to mutter with soft venom about the bull's evil eye and crafty mind. Muriel freshened her smile, then began to hum melodiously to herself as she pitched the tent and set and lit a fire.

Muriel Tree was thirty years old and in no way at all like Aunt Matty in appearance. She had a fine figure, but her breasts and hips were fuller and her waist was thicker. Also she was a head shorter. Although not beautiful, her face had a certain mature prettiness – with big green eyes, a finely chiselled nose between high cheek-bones, a full mouth and a dimpled chin. It was a round face free from blemishes with an evenly tanned complexion that provided a vivid contrast with her lightly spun, short cut, naturally blonde hair. The quiet smile sat well upon such features as she went about her chores, attending to the sleeping quarters and preparing a meal while Aunt Matty saw to it that the animals were provided with food and water.

They did these routine duties on a rota basis, exchanging chores each night. How many nights had it been now, Muriel wondered idly as she pared vegetables and dropped them into the pot with the diced beef. She couldn't remember. There had been so many since she had driven the wagon out of the yard and taken Aunt Matty's advice.

*'Don't look back, my dear. It won't help the way you feel. Afterwards, if you think it's wise, you can come back.'*

'Your heart's on your sleeve again, Muriel!' Aunt Matty said sharply, speaking in reality instead of imagination.

Muriel looked up, startled. She discovered the stew was only half prepared and she hurried to finish it, no longer smiling or humming. Aunt Matty lowered herself sedately to the ground beside the fire and extended her splayed hands towards the flames. Not until she felt the warmth, did she realise how cold the night air had become.

'Do I have to give you my time heals all things lecture again?' she asked after a long pause in which the crackle of the fire was the only sound.

No, Aunt Matty,' Muriel replied solemnly. 'I know it off by heart now. I just hope everything you've told me about Barnaby's memory turns out to be true.'

The older woman sighed and pursed her lips. 'Texas is still a long way off, my dear. I told you that maybe it'd take the whole trip to work.'

Muriel dropped the final piece of carrot into the stew and hung the pot on the tripod. Then she managed a wan smile. 'At least I didn't cry this time, did I?'

Aunt Matty's grin was a lot broader. 'So it's starting to work already. I been called an old witch more times than I care to recall. Maybe that's what I am. I reckon I've got the powers.'

The younger woman's smile developed into a husky laugh. 'But you can't cast a spell on the bull.'

Aunt Matty stroked the hairs growing from the group of moles and formed her unattractive features into the lines of a mock frown. 'Never thought about that, Mu. It's one hell of an idea.'

They both laughed then and the sounds of their happiness echoed off the wall of rock towering above them. Soon, the water in the pot began to give off steam and the vapour carried an appetising aroma of the cooking meat and vegetables. There was some mending to do and Aunt Matty attended to this, putting on a pair of wire-framed spectacles before she took out her work box from behind the seat of the wagon. Then Muriel went to the wagon and climbed aboard to reach inside. She brought out two ivory-gripped Colt .44 revolvers and a brass-framed Winchester rifle. The older woman looked severely over the tops of her spectacles at the weapons, but said nothing. She hated fire-arms, but acknowledged they were necessary out here in the wilderness. Even if Vic Evans and his men did not show up – and with each day that passed this seemed less likely – there were other dangers which could strike at two women trekking an unescorted trail.

Muriel placed one of the Colts on the ground close to Aunt Matty. She pushed the other revolver into the belt of her long coat. The Winchester she held by its frame as she moved away from the fire, going to the lip of the shelf to peer northwards along the valley. Aunt Matty concentrated on her needlework and did not look up until Muriel returned – by way of the tent from which she took plates and cutlery.

'You know, I really think Evans was all talk.'

The older woman nodded her satisfaction. 'Which goes to show I was right again, doesn't it, my dear?'

'You're always right,' was the happy reply. 'And I love you very much indeed.'

'I been wrong sometimes,' Aunt Matty admitted. 'But never about men.'

A comfortable silence settled between the two women. The older one continued with the darning while the younger peered into the fire – pensive, but not sad. Then, when the stew was cooked, they ate. Coffee was made and, while they drank it, they studied a torn and creased map, endeavouring to pin-point their position. They were content and relaxed.

Then a pebble rattled amid the rocks to the west.

'Oh, my God!' Muriel cried, and snatched up the Winchester. She toppled out of a squat on to her side and then rolled. Prone, she aimed the rifle towards the rocks. Fear blurred her vision.

'Just a jackrabbit, maybe!' Aunt Matty rasped. But she picked up the Colt.

'Who's there?' Muriel called, her voice reedy. She realised suddenly that there was no bullet in the breech of the Winchester. She worked the action. The heavy rifle wavered in its aim.

The response to her demand was the whinny of a horse. Not from any of the stallions though, and the sound brought Aunt Matty's fear out from concealment.

'Answer her or we start shooting!' she yelled. She remained seated, resting the barrel of the revolver in the small vee of her pressed-together knees, gripping the butt with both hands.

'Obliged if you wouldn't do that,' a man replied, his voice an evenly pitched drawl.

Both women raked their guns to the left. But there was just a wall of darkness from where the voice came – solid rock indistinguishable from intangible shadow. No man or horse showed.

'You with Evans?' Muriel demanded, and her fear was less apparent in her voice.

'I'm with me, lady.'

'What do you want?'

'First off I want you to stop pointing those guns at me. I don't like it.'

'Something you can do about that,' Aunt Matty offered sourly. 'Get the hell out of here.'

'That's the second thing I want,' the man in the rocks answered. 'But you're in my way.'

The two women looked briefly at each other, then snapped their attention back towards the rocks.

'You can pass, mister!' Aunt Matty allowed.

'Aim to.'

'So show yourself, dammit!'

'Point the guns someplace else.' There was a note of weary impatience in the voice now. 'Normally only give folks the one warning.'

'And then what do you do?' Aunt Matty taunted with a sneer.

The women saw the muzzle flash an instant before they heard the crack of the rifle shot. He had moved silently from where he had stood when he last spoke. But neither Muriel nor Mathilda Tree was able to adjust the aim of her gun. For the shot had shocked them into rigid immobility. They stared in wide-eyed horror at the coffee mug, which the bullet had lifted from the ground and hurled into the centre of the fire. The stallions snorted fearfully. The big bull went backwards, dragging the wagon several yards on locked wheels.

It was this that vented a scream from Muriel. She sprang

erect, leaving the Winchester on the ground, and sprinted towards the spooked bull.

'Muriel!' the older woman cried, forcing herself upright and grimacing at the pain in her back and legs.

But Muriel reached the rear of the wagon without more shots being fired. She began to talk softly and placatingly to the bull, which soon became calmed, pawing at the ground for a few moments.

'You crazy fool!' Aunt Matty snarled, glaring at the darkness shrouded rocks. 'Look what you nearly did!'

'Yes, you could have injured him!' Muriel snapped over her shoulder as she stroked the thick neck of the bull.

'Could have done a lot of things,' the man replied, and his voice came from the right of where the muzzle flash had stabbed the darkness. There were the metallic sounds of a repeating rifle as the action was pumped. 'Put a hole in a mug is all. Tell the old biddy to point the gun someplace else.'

'Old biddy!' Aunt Matty shrieked, swinging the Colt towards the new position of the man.

'Mathilda!' Muriel snapped, whirling away from the now placid bull. She lunged into a run, curving around the side of the wagon to skid to a halt – directly in the firing line of the Colt, and facing the woman who held it. Aunt Matty was trembling from head to foot with rage. 'Lower the gun, please!' she requested firmly.

There were tears poised to spill from the older woman's dark eyes, showing how deeply the insult had struck. Muriel expressed tacit sympathy and then gave a curt nod. Aunt Matty fought against her emotions and allowed her arm to drop limply to her side. Muriel stepped away so that the man in the rocks could see that the Colt was no longer aimed at him. A clucking sound came from the darkness, then the clop of hooves.

'Mister, you ain't no gentleman to address a lady so!' Aunt Matty snarled, channeling all her rage into her voice.

The visitor to the night camp stepped out from the rocks into the open moonlight. At first, the women saw just his silhouette as he led his horse closer. A tall man rising to at least three inches above six feet. A rangy, loose-limbed frame that he carried with a natural grace. Carrying a rifle that was canted across his left shoulder, a hand wrapped around the frame so that he could snap the gun down to level it at the first hint of trouble. Then he moved into the circle of light thrown by the fire and the two half frightened – half angry women saw him more clearly.

The tall frame, which weighed probably two hundred pounds and was certainly possessed of a great deal of easy strength, was clothed in black; riding boots, levis, shirt and neckerchief. But a lot of grey trail dust clung to the ill-used garb to make his wide-brimmed, low-crowned hat almost a match. The hat was tilted slightly forward on top of a head of long, thick black hair that reached down to brush his shoulders with its ends. The face beneath the hat was as leanly suggestive of power as the body. A face with light, piercing blue eyes that surveyed the world from under hooded lids; above a hawkish nose flanked by high cheekbones: a narrow mouth fashioned to a cruel line, and a firm jaw. His skin was dark, from long exposure to weather or by heritage. Probably the latter or a combination of the two, the women decided. For the form of his features suggested he had a recent ancestry that was a mixture of the Latin and the Aryan. Putting an accurate age to him was difficult. He wore a full day's growth of bristle, that grew thickest along the top and at the corners of his mouth to indicate he wore a moustache. And his skin was deeply scored. But the lines could have been inscribed by hardship rather than mere years. He was somewhere in his thirties, the women decided. For the way he moved was younger than his countenance suggested.

In addition to the Winchester rifle, he carried a single Frontier Colt, which jutted from a holster tied down to his right thigh. The horse he led was a black gelding.

'I said you ain't no gentleman!' Aunt Matty repeated after she and Muriel had been subjeced to an insolent scrutiny by the blue eyes, as cold as mid-winter ice. The women were dressed warmly for the mountain night, their clothes topped by thick coats that enveloped them from throats to midway down their high boots. But both of them had the disconcerting impression that the raking eyes had been able to penetrate clear through to their flesh.

'Wasn't for your soprano voices, wouldn't be able to be so certain about you, ma'am,' the man said. And now there was a faint trace of humour in the set of his thin lips. It robbed his mouthline of its cruelty, but failed to take the ice from his eyes – eyes that looked incapable of expressing any emotion, unless it be hatred.

He had halted close to the fire, on the opposite side to where the women stood. The light was brighter there and they could see traces of blueness through the bristles and ingrained dirt on his face. He slid the Winchester into the saddleboot and dropped the reins so that he was able to extend both hands towards the warmth of the blaze.

'We dress according to the weather, mister!' Aunt Matty replied sternly and there was no longer anger in her voice or expression. She was studying the man with the same brand of arrogance he had shown when appraising her.

'Wise, ma'am,' the man allowed with a nod. He dropped down on to his haunches so that he could put his face closer to the heat.

'You're mighty polite all of a sudden.'

'Ain't polite to point a gun at a man, ma'am. I treat folks the way they treat me.' He rubbed his long-fingered, dark-skinned hands together, relishing the warmth.

Aunt Matty made a sound of disgust deep in her throat. 'What do you expect us to do?' she demanded. 'Two women alone in camp when a strange man approaches?'

'I ain't two women,' he replied evenly.

Muriel trusted herself to speak at last. 'I don't care who or what you are,' she said, still angry but keeping her voice under control. 'All I know is that you aren't welcome here. You said you wanted to pass, why don't you?'

The man swung his attention from the old woman to the young one and his impassive expression gave no indication that he was impressed by her green-eyed prettiness. He nodded. 'No sweat, ladies. Obliged you let me use your fire this long.'

He straightened.

'Seems to me you helped yourself, mister,' Aunt Matty snapped, and made another throaty sound of disgust.

The man's mouthline tightened again. He dipped a hand into a pocket of his pants, took out a dime and flicked it across the fire. It dropped between the two women. 'For the kindling I used,' he growled, and swung to slide a boot into a stirrup. 'I always pay my way.'

'We didn't mean for you to . . . ' Muriel started.

'Muriel!' Aunt Matty cut in severely as the man swung astride the gelding. 'Don't you go apologising to this drifter. Not after he insulted me without saying he was sorry.'

'Still the same old tough egg, Mathilda!'

The words were shouted from the lip of the shelf. The man astride the gelding saw horror leap across the faces of the women as he swung his head to look back over his shoulder.

'Evans!' Muriel screamed.

Aunt Matty started to bring up the Colt. Four men appeared at the lip of the shelf, rifles aimed from their shoulders. From the corner of his eye, the man on the gelding saw two more men lunge out of the rocks from where he had approached the campsite. But they carried lariats instead of rifles. The ropes were whirled high and released.

'No killin'!' a man yelled. The same voice as before.

Four rifles exploded a fusillade of shots. Three bullets smashed into the heart of the fire and sprayed burning embers out the far side. The fourth clanged against the cooking pot and ricocheted. It spun end-over-end into the panic-widened right eye of the gelding. The horse leapt backwards and toppled to the side. The man's expression hardened but he made no sound as he kicked his feet clear of the stirrups and lunged clear of the saddle, sliding the Winchester from the boot as he hit the ground. But there were plenty of other sounds to echo off the cliff face in the wake of the rifle shots.

The bull, spooked for the second time within a few minutes, was snorting wildly as he struggled against the pull of his tether and the two lariats which were noosed around his thick neck. The stallions were venting their own fear as they reared against the restraint of hobbling lines. And the two women were screaming. Aunt Matty with pain as she beat at the flames which had erupted as the hot embers fell on her coat and in her hair; Muriel with horror as she dragged the older woman to the ground and flung herself on top of the struggling form.

'Drop the friggin' gun, tall man!'

The voice of another attacker, came from the rocky area to the east as the man whirled beside his dead horse to rake his Winchester along the line of four riflemen. He froze his body, but turned his head. Three more men with rifles had stepped into open moonlight.

'Do like he says, mister.' This was from the one Muriel had called Evans. 'Or I'll change what I said about no killin'.'

The narrow blue eyes, glittering between their narrowed lids, returned their level gaze to the obvious boss of the bunch. 'There's already been killing,' he said icily. 'My horse ain't going to get up.'

The flames which had threatened Mathilda Tree were out and the only sounds to come from the two women now were sobs. The horses had quietened and the bull's anger had calmed to a point where he merely breathed heavily through his flared dripping nostrils.

'Horses don't count!' Evans snarled.

He was close to six feet tall, with broad shoulders, a wide chest and a bulbous stomach. He had a good looking face decorated with a bushy black moustache. He was about fifty. Like his men, who were all younger, he was dressed in a sheepskin jacket, low-crowned hat, levis and riding boots. But he also wore ear-muffs. All the men looked well-fed and well-rested.

'I can, feller. I only had but the one horse. Now I don't have any.'

Evans advanced, ignoring the Winchester which was aimed at him: confident of his cover. 'You've only got but the one life, too,' he pointed out. He halted and injected a heavier tone into his voice. 'Drop the rifle and keep it.'

The Winchester remained in a rock-steady aim on his chest,

left of centre. But Evans was not looking at the gun. Instead, he found his deep-set eyes trapped by the level stare of the man behind the gun. And, in the icy blueness of the stare, he saw a readiness to kill him. Fear made subtle inroads into his confidence. The men behind him moved forward. The three at the side shuffled closer. Those who had roped the bull dropped their free hands to drape the butts of the holstered revolvers jutting from under their coats.

'Don't provoke him, stranger!' Aunt Matty advised, nodding to Muriel that she was all right as she sat up. 'Vic Evans is nothing but a mean, murdering skunk!'

Evans started to express anger, but then a quizzical look became set on his face. 'Stranger? You mean you ain't here to protect these two females?'

The man beside the dead horse maintained the steady stare and the unwavering aim. 'If I was, feller, you and your bunch wouldn't have got within a half mile of here.'

'Talks up a storm, don't he?' one of the men behind Evans said harshly.

'Shuddup!' Evans snarled. Then he worked a personable smile on to his face and lowered his rifle until it pointed at the ground. 'Puts a different complexion on things, mister . . . ?'

'Edge,' came the soft-spoken reply.

'Edge? Just that?'

'It's gotten to be enough for me.'

Evans shrugged, then waved his free hand, palm down. All the levelled rifles were lowered. 'Like I was saying, Mr Edge. That makes a difference. My quarrel's with the Tree women. See, they stole that there bull from me and – '

'It was Barnaby's bull!' Muriel snapped.

'Damn right!' the older woman agreed.

Edge tipped the Winchester to cant it across his left shoulder. He spat and the globule of moisture hit the ground midway between himself and Evans. 'Ain't one for talking bull,' he growled. 'Right now, it's horsetalk interests me.'

Evans glowered at the women, then smiled at Edge. 'Just so, sir. What happened to your mount was an unfortunate accident. Made more regrettable since you are nothing but an innocent bystander. Two of my men will ride double and you may take the pick of our horses. How does that suit?'

'Don't trust the bastards, mister!' Aunt Matty warned.

'We could have a deal,' Edge allowed, ignoring the women as Evans glared at her.

'Brad!' the big man called, still smarting with anger at the insult. 'Take Mr Edge down to where Jeb's got the horses. And see he gets what he wants.'

'Sure, Mr Evans,' one of the men behind the big man acknowledged. He stepped forward and jerked a thumb. 'This way, bud.'

'Don't say I didn't warn you!' Aunt Matty growled.

'What does it matter?' Muriel asked sullenly. 'Forget him, Mathilda. He wouldn't help us.'

'You're right,' the older woman agreed with resignation. Then she glared hatred at Edge as he followed the man named Brad. 'Just helps himself.'

'To a little warmth is all,' Edge responded lightly. 'And I paid.'

'Hope you had your ten centsworth,' Aunt Matty muttered, brushing a lock of singed hair from in front of her eyes.

Edge showed a wry grin as he glanced around at the riflemen. 'Good value,' he said. 'When a dime buys this much heat.'

# Chapter Two

THE slender, gimlet-eyed Brad led Edge around the three men who had covered the east flank of the campsite, and through a gap in the rocks on to a natural trail by which the rig had been hauled up on to the shelf.

'You got any more nasty names you want to call me, Mathilda?' the two men heard Evans snarl.

'Please!' Muriel said shrilly. 'Just take what you came for and go. Leave us alone.'

Edge saw Brad glance suspiciously at him as he drew level with his designated guide.

'Mr Evans won't leave it at that, bud.'

Edge rasped his free hand over his stubbled jaw, noting that Brad had his right hand draped over the butt of his holstered Remington. 'So?'

'So I sure hope you're as cold and mean as you look, bud. Ain't your trouble.'

Edge sighed, raking his narrow eyes over the side of the rocky valley into which they were strolling. He spotted a bunch of horses standing placidly under an overhang of rock about a half-mile distant. 'Only got the one problem, feller,' he said softly.

'What's that?' Brad asked, fast and suspicious.

'Making sure I get me a good horse.'

Up at the campsite, the two men with the lariats moved in close to the bull, talking softly to the animal to keep him calm. Evans approached the women with a cruel smile turning up the corners of his mouth beneath the moustache. The five riflemen ambled over to block escape to the side. The cliff face barred the way behind Aunt Matty and Muriel. But neither woman showed any inclination to run. They were frightened, but there was a certain dignity in the way they held their ground.

'Names won't hurt you, Evans!' Aunt Matty taunted, her face made uglier by the yellow blisters which the flames had raised on the wrinkled flesh. 'And anyway, there's nothing I can call you which you don't already know you are.'

Evans halted three feet in front of the women, his stare fixed on Aunt Matty. His eyes smiled to match his mouth. 'You've always had a nasty tongue, Mathilda,' he accused softly 'Always speaking ugly words. On account of that apology for a face, I guess.'

'She sure ain't no beauty, Mr Evans,' a pasty-faced boy of about eighteen said with a high-pitched laugh.

'A mule's ass is better lookin' than she is,' another man said.

Evans broadened his smile as the men voiced their appreciation of the comment. Then he held up a hand and the sounds of the humour were immediately curtailed. Muriel saw the evil lurking behind the smile and she swallowed hard.

'Go!' she implored. 'Take the bull and go. Please.'

Evans swung his head towards her and the latent evil sprang to the surface as rage suffused his features with a dark red, shading into purple at the centres of his cheeks. 'Hold your damn tongue, woman!' he snarled. 'You got grief for an excuse, but I ain't allowin' you no more leeway on that.'

He brought up his Winchester until it was aimed at Muriel's belly. She paled until the smoke smudges on her cheek, jaw and forehead looked almost three dimensional against the bloodless background.

'You goin' to kill us like you did Barnaby?' Aunt Matty taunted.

'Mr Evans!' another man with a moustache put in nervously. He was short and fat, with a round face and prominent teeth.

'Shuddup, George!' Evans told him, without taking his eyes off Muriel, whose fear had expanded to the brink of terror. Then he moderated his tone. 'No, I don't figure to do any killin' – unless I have to. But I'll surely blast the grievin' widow here if you don't do like I say, Mathilda.'

Muriel gasped and reached out a trembling hand. It was taken in the firm grasp of the older woman.

'What's that, Evans?' Aunt Matty asked her voice still strong.

Evans smiled again, maintaining his concentration on the younger woman. 'Always felt sickened just looking at that apology for a face you've got, Mathilda. Ever since I known you, and that's been a long time.'

'You ain't never improved in all the years!' she retorted.

Evans went on as if the interruption had never happened. 'But I always did have a hankerin' to see how Mother Nature made it up to you.'

Disgust spread across the ugly features.

'Please leave?' Muriel begged.

'Strip!' Evans barked.

'Yiippppeee!' the skinny youngster yelled gleefully.

'I'll go along with that, Mr Evans,' George said eagerly, shedding his former nervousness. 'She got five men to the preacher with that body of hers.'

'Must really be somethin',' a man with a hare-lip put in. 'All of 'em died with the heart attack.'

'Yeah!' exclaimed a man with a broken nose. 'And all in bed at that!'

'Now we don't know if it really was while they was at that!' one of the men in charge of the bull yelled.

'Get your damn clothes off!' Evans bellowed across the burst of laughter.

'No!' Muriel shrieked.

She made to lunge at their tormentor, but Aunt Matty jerked her back. Evans snarled and thrust the Winchester forward. The muzzle jabbed Muriel hard in the stomach and she sat down, the air rasping out of her.

'*Yes*, my dear,' the older woman disagreed as she released Muriel's hand and raised her arms to start to unfasten her coat buttons. Utter contempt showed in her dark eyes as she stared at Evans. 'If it will save our lives.'

Edge and Brad were almost at the horses. But, because the cliff face prevented the noise escaping the valley, they were able to hear the raucous laughter and the loudest of the shouting voices.

'Seems we're missin' all the fun,' the slightly-built Brad muttered discontentedly. 'The old bitch sure riled up Vic Evans.'

'Ain't hard to do, I'd guess.'

Brad nodded. 'How'd you feel if a couple of women stole a fifty thousand dollar bull off you, bud?' he asked rhetorically.

Only by a fractional narrowing of his already slitted eyes did Edge betray his surprise at the statement. 'Guess I'd feel I had something to beef about,' he admitted.

'Who's there?' a man called sharply.

Brad groaned. 'President friggin' Grant come to give you a friggin' medal for friggin' bravery!' he snarled.

'Brad?'

Edge's guide spat. 'Yeah, Jeb. And a guy who's gonna take one of our nags. If we let him!'

The half-breed was looking at a fat man who had stepped from out of the shadows, a rifle levelled from the hip but aimed wide. As the final four words were snapped out, he half-turned, whipping down the Winchester and poised to power into a crouch.

'No chance, bud!'

Somewhere along the line, as they had covered the final stretch from the shelf to the place where the horses were waiting. Brad had eased his Remington from its holster. He had kept the drawn gun hidden at the side of his body. Now it was in full sight, after he had pivoted slightly and raised it to the aim, cocking it in the same smooth series of actions.

Edge froze, his lean face impassive. His eyes stared fixedly at the hand fisted around the Remington. It was here that the first sign of a shot would show. Jeb was an unknown quantity, beyond the fact that he was nervy. He could be panicked into firing: or simply be too scared to do anything unless he had specific instructions. A single second seemed to be stretched into a long, tense minute. No guns exploded sound. Up at the campsite on the shelf, the firelight glowed red in reflection on the cliff face. Gigantic shadows moved against the splash of dull crimson.

'Horses don't count he said,' Edge reminded softly.

'Evans horses do, bud,' Brad countered.

'What the hell is this about, Brad?' Jeb demanded. 'There weren't supposed to be no killin'.'

'Ain't been, yet.' His gimlet eyes were fixed on Edge's face.

'About to be?' the half-breed asked.

'Same as back there, bud. Drop the rifle and no one gets hurt.'

Edge switched his attention to Brad's tense face and knew he was no killer. A ranch-hand, maybe. Like Jeb and the other men who took orders from Vic Evans. A bunch of cowboys pressed into doing unaccustomed work for their boss. The kind who could handle guns but who would never use them to kill, unless in self-defence. He looked away from the man and back towards the firelit shelf at the south end of the valley. Gusts of laughter, whoops of glee and yells of encouragement sounded from there. But no sounds of anybody getting killed.

'I don't want no part in any shootin' play!' Jeb whined.

Edge loosened his grip around the frame of the Winchester and the rifle clattered to the hard ground. 'I'm with him,' he told Brad. 'Dying ain't my scene.'

Brad showed a grin that was largely of relief. 'Smart, bud.'

Edge grimaced. 'Most times I get that way quicker, feller.'

Up on the shelf of rock, Mathilda Tree stood naked in the flickering light of the fire. The watching men had become suddenly quiet, to the extent that they held their breath for long moments. Apart from the crackle of flames attacking the wood, the only sound beneath the towering cliff face came from Muriel. As the disrobing woman removed the final garment, Muriel had covered her face with her hands and began to sob into her palms.

It was the final act of the enforced strip which had silenced the eager men. The woman at whom they stared in tacit awe had worn a one-piece undergarment. As she slid the straps off her shoulders, it fell down the length of her body to settle around her ankles. She did not step out of it. She did not move at all. Instead, she gazed along the darkness-shrouded valley, every part of her face and body flushing to a deep scarlet as she submitted to the dumbfounded scrutiny of the men watching her. And, although she did not look at one of the surprised faces, she sensed their mood change yet again. First there had been wild hilarity – then awe. Now lust was created deep within the men and began to implant the glint of desire in their eyes. For Mathilda Tree's body was all she claimed it to be.

Smooth and firm, with high, small, conical breasts; a narrow waist that needed no foundation garment to maintain its line; a flat stomach between the flare of hips; and finely-shaped, slender thighs surmounted by a rich growth of dark hair at her pubes. There was not a blue vein, a wrinkle or the trace of loose flesh anywhere. It was, indeed, the body of a young girl under the face of an aging harridan.

'Jesus, will you look at that!' the skinny youngster breathed.

'I'm lookin', I'm lookin',' George squeaked.

'Mr Evans?' the man with the harelip said, and there was a tone of pleading in his voice.

Other men muttered, to themselves and to their neighbours. It was as if Evans was the final man to regain his composure. He had to clear his throat.

'Mathilda, you surely got compensated,' he said huskily. 'When I used to see you parading around town like a girl fresh out of school, I figured it was all done with stays and such.'

'Have you seen enough?' Aunt Matty asked, still staring into infinity. Her voice was reedy with pent-up emotion.

'Oh, yes!' Muriel moaned, still hiding her face in her hands. 'Yes. Please say yes. Please go and leave us alone!'

'Seen enough!' Evans snarled, his voice back to a normal pitch. 'But I ain't done enough.'

'No, sir!' the skinny younster rasped.

'Clint?' Vic Evans snapped.

'I get first crack?' the boy asked in high excitement.

'See if there's a sack in the wagon,' somebody suggested. 'Put over that lousy face.'

Evans trapped Aunt Matty's gaze to his by the sheer will-power he generated in his eyes. The woman looked from infinity to the man and reacted to the shouts of the others. Tears welled up in her eyes and coursed down the scored flesh of her cheeks.

'Shuddup!' Evans bellowed, and the order clamped silence over the campsite. Even Muriel stopped weeping and peered out through the cracks between her fingers. 'We ain't no depraved rapists!' he roared, swinging his head from side to side to glower at the abruptly contrite men. Then he looked back at Aunt Matty. 'You want to apologise for those names you called me, Mathilda?'

Aunt Matty swallowed hard. 'I'm sorry,' she whispered.

'Louder!'

'I'm sorry!'

The man nodded and showed a grin of pure pleasure. 'That's good, Mathilda,' he complimented. 'But to be really sorry you ought to wear sackcloth and ashes.' He laughed. 'You already did the ashes, though, didn't you?'

'That's a hot one, Mr Evans,' somebody called.

But no one laughed. Having humiliated Mathilda Tree, the men were now suffering self-contempt for what they had taken part in – and what they had intended to do before Evans pulled them back from the brink.

'But I got this other idea, Mathilda. Clint?'

'Yes, sir, Mr Evans?'

'There's a bucket hung under the wagon son. Get it and take it over to the bull. See if the animal got anything off his mind, you know what I mean?'

'I guess so, Mr Evans,' the younster replied miserably, moving to obey the order.

There was silence again, as Clint did what was asked of him. As he carried the half-filled bucket back to Evans, he kept his face averted from the foul stench rising from its contents. He set his burden down beside his boss and hurriedly withdrew. Evans made small clicking sounds with his tongue on the roof of his mouth as he put down his rifle and lifted the bucket. He took two paces which put him immediately in front of the naked woman. She became rigid, clenching her fists and screwing her eyes tight closed. He raised the bucket high, stretching forward so that it was held directly above the naked woman. Then, turning it away from himself so that he wasn't splashed by the fresh, moist bull excrement, Evans up-ended the bucket.

With a cruel grin deforming his lips beneath the bushy moustache, Evans watched the evil-smelling mess cling amid the dyed hair and crawl over the aged face to drop on to the smooth shoulders.

'Now you're really what I always said you were, Mathilda!' Aunt Matty's tormentor growled. 'Nothin' but a shithead.'

Clint giggled.

'Lets' get outta here, Mr Evans,' the fat George whined.

Some of the other men nodded or made sounds of agreement. Others looked with admiration at the stoic dignity with which the naked old woman suffered her defilation. She continued to stand erect. And now she was immobile to the extent that she did not breathe.

'Think about it, Mathilda!' Evans said, angry at the lack of response from the woman he had humiliated. 'In private!'

These last two words were snarled at Aunt Matty as he slammed the bucket down over her head. Then he whirled away from her and stooped to snatch up his Winchester.

'Clint, take their guns!' he ordered.

The skinny youngster scampered forward and gathered up the two fancy-grip Colts and the Winchester. Overpowered by the stench and lack of air, Aunt Matty surrendered to a faint and cork-screwed to the ground. Muriel vented a cry of despair.

'Kill me if you want!' she screamed at Evans, and lunged

to Aunt Matty's side, to wrench off the bucket.

'No killin', Mrs Tree,' the grim-faced Evans reminded. 'But that only goes for this time. Me and the boys are goin' to deliver my bull to the man who wants him. You and Mathilda try to steal him again, and I'll blast you into the same hell Barnaby's at. You hear me, woman?'

Muriel was using Aunt Matty's discarded dress to wipe the mess from the ugly face. The thunderous tone with which the question was put forced her to look up at the tall man towering above her. 'I hear you,' she whispered.

Evans nodded and strode to the lip of the shelf. He cupped his hands around his mouth. 'Brad! You taken care of that saddletramp?'

His voice powered along the dark valley.

'He ain't gonna be no trouble!' came the response.

Evans glanced around at his men and nodded his head towards the gap in the rocks that was the start of the way down. Then he strode purposefully into the gap and his men followed, the two with the lariats urging the big bull into movement. Only the stricken-faced George held back, taking a curved course to pass close by the two women. Muriel had covered Aunt Matty's nakedness with the long coat.

'I'm sorry this happened, Mrs Tree,' George said softly. 'Tell Mathilda I said it.'

'She don't have to,' Aunt Matty growled, surprising both Muriel and George – by the fact of her return to awareness and by the venom in her tone. 'Go and join the rest of the skunks, George Frimley. You smell worse than I do.'

George looked at the hatred in the face under the filth. Then he turned and lunged into a lumbering run to catch up with the others.

Down under the rocky overhang where the horses were gathered, Edge was seated on the ground in reasonable comfort. His back was resting against the smooth curve of a boulder. His ankles were tied together and his wrists were bound in front of his body. He wore an impassive expression as he watched the group of men approach.

'Not so tough as he looks, uh?' Evans asked with a tight grin.

'Easy meat,' Brad answered, smiling proudly.

The overweight Jeb swallowed hard. He held two Winchesters – his own and Edge's – and had the half-breed's gunbelt with its holstered Colt draped over his shoulder. 'I don't think so, Mr Evans,' he countered nervously, darting out a tongue to lick his lips. 'Reckons he's gonna kill Brad for takin' his guns. And reckons he'll kill any of the rest of us who aims a gun at him a second time.'

'Talks up a storm, don't he?' Brad taunted.

Evans grimaced as he approached Edge. A flicker of doubt showed on his face as he met the steady gaze of the ice-blue eyes. But he was able to lose it by turning his attention to the loose knots in the rope holding the wrists together. He grunted his approval and turned to go to the horses.

'Mount up,' he instructed. As the men complied, Evans looked back at Edge. From long range, the intensity of the half-breed's stare was not so effective. 'Can understand how you feel, mister,' he called. 'You're what they call an innocent bystander. Got caught up in other folk's business. But count your blessin's. Lost a horse and a couple of guns. Can't give you one of these horses on account of me and the boys have got a long ride ahead of us. We'll check your guns with the sheriff at the next town south. Keepin' them so you don't get any ideas about trailin' us for revenge or somethin' like that. Brad's tied you so it won't be too hard to get loose. Yes, sir. Count your blessin's I'm a man only takes what's his.'

'Figure you'll get yours, feller,' Edge answered wryly as Evans heeled his horse forward and his men fell in behind him. The two who brought up the rear were leading the fifty thousand dollar bull.

Dust rose under the hooves and drifted in the air towards Edge. A lot of it settled on to him. Veiled from any backward glances by the southbound riders, Edge raised his wrists which had been tied together and leaned forward to push his head through the vee of his arms. His long fingers probed between his hair and under his shirt collar. As he straightened, knocking off his hat, an open straight razor was gripped between the thumb and forefinger of his right hand. He moved the razor towards his face and clenched the wooden handle between his teeth. The finely honed blade sliced through his wrist bonds as though the rope was no stronger than rotted thread. The rope at his ankles parted just as easily and he stood up, retrieving his hat and pushing the razor back into the leather pouch that hung on a beaded cord at the nape of his neck.

He could no longer see the riders after the dust had settled, but he could hear their progress through the rock-strewn southern exit of the valley. They were moving at a canter. He wasted no time staring southwards for a futile glimpse of them. Instead, using his neckerchief to wipe the dust from his face, he ambled in the wake of the men. Then he veered towards the west, heading up the slope which led to the campsite on the shelf. The position of the night camp was not so clearly marked any longer, now that the fire had burned low. But, on the shelf, the glowing embers gave adequate light to show the wagon, the four horses and the tent. The women were nowhere to be seen. The dead horse was.

'Hey!' he called into the hard silence which had clamped down now that the sound of hoof-beats had faded. 'We've already done the bit with the guns, right ladies?'

'Edge?' From inside the tent. The voice of Aunt Matty.

'Yeah.'

'Go away and leave us alone!' the younger woman wailed. She sounded close to hysteria.

'No!' Aunt Matty called quickly. The tent flap was flung aside and she crawled out and rose erect, holding her long coat tightly around her. Below the hem her ankles and feet were bare. Her garishly blonde hair was limp and stringy with wetness. It framed a face set in rigid lines of grim determination.

Edge strolled casually into the diminished glow of the fire. 'Like to buy one of your horses and one of your guns, ma'am,' he said.

'Lousy skunks took our guns, too,' the old woman answered flatly. 'And our horses ain't for sale.'

Edge pursed his lips, noting that in at least one respect, Mathilda Tree and Vic Evans were alike. When they were riled, their veneers of genteelness were shed and they talked like barflies. 'Pay you a high price.'

'No deal!' Aunt Matty snapped. 'I already paid a high price to keep what that bastard left me. And I aim to use it to see him and the skunks he rides with pay higher than me.'

'No!' Muriel cried, crawling from the tent and pulling herself erect. Her face was puffy from crying, and misery sharpened her terror. 'We're going home.'

Edge dropped to his haunches at the side of his dead gelding and began to unfasten the cinch and bridle. Although the fire was almost out, he welcomed the warmth of the embers.

'Mr Edge?' Aunt Matty snapped.

'Yes, ma'am?'

'What would you do if a man filled a bucket with cowdung and tipped it over your head?' she demanded. 'After first stripping you naked?'

'Kill him, first chance I got.'

Aunt Matty nodded emphatically. 'That is precisely what I intend to do.'

Edge stood up, dragging the saddle out from under the carcase of the horse. 'He's yours ma'am,' he allowed.

'And the others. They have equal guilt.'

Edge shook his head. 'Not the feller called Brad. He stole my guns.'

Aunt Matty seemed ready to argue. But then she gave an unladylike grunt. 'Very well. Since we share a common goal, you may ride on the wagon with us.'

Muriel looked from Edge to Aunt Matty and back again. Her shoulders drooped as she conceded defeat to their argument. 'Like one big, revenge-bent family,' she rasped, soft and sour.

Edge spat as he turned to carry his saddle and bridle towards the wagon. Then he looked back over his shoulder and showed a cold grin. 'We all came from Adam and Eve, so could be we're kissing-cousins,' he drawled.

'I don't want to travel with him!' Muriel pleaded.

'Well, you're gonna!' Aunt Matty countered severely.

Edge made the grin broader and colder. 'Damn right. A family that slays together stays together.'

# Chapter Three

'I AIN'T really Muriel's aunt,' Mathilda Tree said as Edge drove the wagon out on to a stage trail. 'Just calls me Aunt Matty on account of I'm a lot older than she is.'

They had been rolling for an hour after breaking camp. The going had been hard and slow, the broken terrain dictating the pace; unless they were prepared to risk a horse snapping a leg, or a busted axle. Neither of the women had objected to Edge taking the reins. The only argument was between the women: about which of them should take the limited space inside and which rode up on the seat with the half-breed. Edge settled it by flipping the dime which had been returned to him. Aunt Matty won and ordered the sullen Muriel to climb into the rear and try to get some rest on a broken-up hay bale.

Then the grim-faced older woman had climbed up beside Edge and watched him closely over the first mile or so. The half-breed was conscious of her silent scrutiny of him, but he did not allow this to affect the way he drove. He handled the team and wagon expertly, making the best time possible and sticking steadfastly to the clear tracks left by the bunch of horsemen and the bull. This was what the woman was checking on: ensuring that Edge did not act recklessly in his eagerness to catch up with the quarry.

He was aware when she gave him her approval, even though

no word was spoken. For the rigidity went out of her slender body and her ugly face relaxed slightly. But then, with nothing to occupy her mind, it became obvious that the verbal silence was beginning to irk her. And, as soon as they cut on to the trail that curved south east across a broad plateau featured with outcrops and clumps of mesquite and cactus plants, she could hold her peace no longer.

'That so?' Edge replied indifferently, after he had raked his narrow-eyed gaze over the country ahead and failed to spot any sign of movement. But disturbed dust told him he was rolling the rig in the right direction. A flick of the reins spurred the team from a walk to a canter and the horses obeyed without reluctance. A fast pace would help to combat the increasing chill of the night air.

'Sure is, mister. We're really sisters-in-law. She married my kid brother Barnaby. I was married to my last husband at the time. My fifth. You married?'

'No.'

'Was once. I can tell. I know men.' She sniffed. 'Remember how I told you not to trust Evans?'

'Sure.' He spat over the side of the seat. 'I was married. Forget it. I have.' His gaze became colder than the night as he stared ahead over the bouncing backs of the team. 'Few days ago a guy brought back the memory.'

'Rough, uh?' Aunt Matty asked, her tone sympathetic.

'On him, lady. He died.' His voice was as cold as his eyes.

Aunt Matty shivered and could not be certain it was entirely caused by a light, but biting breeze which sprang across the plateau. She huddled down deeper into her coat anyway, and turned up the collar.

'Like I was sayin', mister,' she continued after a full minute had slipped by. 'Muriel, she married my kid brother Barnaby. He wasn't much of a catch. Not like my fifth, who died just six days after Muriel and Barnaby was wed. Hey, you listening?'

'Does it matter?' Edge asked, not looking at her.

'It does. I'd like you to know Mu and me didn't steal that bull – not really.'

'Between you and Evans, ma'am. None of my business.'

Aunt Matty blew into her cupped hands. She sniffed again. 'Well, I'm gonna tell you anyway. Even if it just means that flapping my mouth keeps my lips from freezing together.'

Edge sighed. 'Sure, ma'am.'

Aunt Matty gave a grim-faced, triumphant nod. And continued with her story. 'Barnaby got the family farm after our father died. Right up in the far north on the Canadian border. Let it go all to hell while he wasted his time gambling and cross-breeding beef. Only it turns out that the cross-breeding stuff wasn't a waste of time after all.'

The stage trail snaked between a small mesa and a pinnacle of rock and the huddled buildings of a town showed in the distance. They were on a rise and the elevation enabled Edge and the woman to see the twin silver threads of a railroad arrowing away from the south side of the town. A few pinpricks of yellow light against the bulky blackness of the buildings competed with the stars sprinkled overhead.

'Mu and me were closer than we thought,' Aunt Matty said absently. Then she strengthened her tone. 'Barnaby had this English cow and a French bull. He put them together and that beast you saw was the result. Put on more than five pounds a day while he was growing. Full grown now and weighs better than three and a half thousand pounds. That's a lot of bull, uh?'

'Aint saying nothing,' Edge answered evenly.

'So to hell with you, mister. I'll cut the story short in case I bore you into goin' to sleep. There's a rancher down in Texas named Woodrow Ryan. He's been trying to breed that kinda bull for years, but he never got lucky. He heard about what Barnaby did and telegraphed an offer of fifty thousand dollars if the beast was all it was cracked up to be. But the offer come a little late. Barnaby got into a poker game with Evans and two of his hands. They took him for what little money he had and egged him into putting up the bull as collateral for a loan. Evans beat him and foreclosed.'

'Man who invented poker's got a lot to answer for,' Edge answered flatly.

'So's the man who thought of marking cards,' Aunt Matty growled.

'Cold deck, uh?'

Aunt Matty shivered. 'Colder than this damn night.'

They had rolled to within a mile of the town now, and the wagon rattled past a sign: *Railton – Elevation 7000 ft.*

'Soon as Barnaby found out about it, he went to get his bull back. Evans ordered him off his spread. Barnaby was a no-account fool to the end. He said he wouldn't leave without the animal. Evans and those nine hands of his you saw tonight – they all drew at once and the mortician had to dig ten bullets outta Barnaby before we buried the body in the yard of the family farm.'

'All that lead,' Edge said softly. 'Pretty heavy argument that the bull belongs to Evans.'

'Muriel didn't go for it, mister, 'specially after the judge reckoned Barnaby got what he deserved and he weren't gonna single out any of the ten men to even slap a label of what he called justifiable homicide on.'

Railton had just the one street. Flanked by darkened houses at the north end where Edge angled the wagon to the side and reined the team to a halt. But a dozen lamps glowed at the other end, where the street broadened out into a square in front of the railroad depot. A train was backed into the depot. Immediately behind a Mogul locomotive which was beginning to build up steam, were three passenger cars alongside a raised boardwalk. Behind these were two loaded flatcars and a boxcar with a brake wagon on the tail. The freight cars of the train were in the penned stockyard section of the depot.

Kerosene lamps hung on posts, clearly illuminated the scene as Evans's men attempted to drive the reluctant white bull up a ramp and into the boxcar. Evans himself seemed to be having an argument with a slightly built man in a dark uniform and peaked cap. The hiss of escaping steam covered all the other sounds in the vicinity of the depot. After the wagon had come to rest, the remainder of the town was silent save for the low howl of the strengthening wind between the buildings.

'Muriel!' Aunt Matty called tensely as Edge wound the reins around the brake lever.

There was movement in the rear of the wagon. 'Where are we?' the younger woman asked, with a yawn.

'Where we were headed. Railton. And them skunks are puttin' the animal on the train just like we figured to do.'

There was a scuffling, a thud and a soft cry as Muriel Tree climbed out of the wagon and dropped to the ground, hurting herself in the process. Edge climbed down easily from the seat and saw Muriel limping towards him.

'What are you contemplating on doing, mister?' Aunt Matty demanded.

Muriel was staring along the street towards the lamplit scene at the depot. Her pretty face was still recovering from the effects of interrupted sleep, but she had obviously done a great deal of thinking before she took her rest. For she was expressing the same kind of grim determination the older woman had shown back at the campsite. She in no way looked as if she intended to go home and forget what had happened now.

Edge was also surveying Railton, but was ignoring the depot. He had seen as much as he wanted of it. Instead, his hooded eyes sought a sign to indicate the location of the law office. He spotted it, with a low level of light filtering through a window beneath it.

'Like my marriage, lady,' he answered flatly and moved away from the wagon.

'What does he mean, Aunt Matty?' Muriel asked, watching the tall, lean figure move gracefully along the side of the resting team.

'Means it's none of our business,' came the soft voiced reply.

Muriel looked at her sister-in-law now, anxiety replacing the former determination. 'What are we going to do?'

'Keep our fingers crossed that tall hunk of meanness cuts down our opposition some, my dear,' the older woman replied coldly.

Edge didn't hear the exchange. The women had served their purpose by providing him with transport. Now they were behind him and immediately out of his mind. Nothing he saw during frequent glances at the depot caused him to quicken his pace. Three and a half thousand pounds'-worth of obstinate bull could not be hurried: and the more aggressive his handlers became, the less inclined the animal was to enter the boxcar. The locomotive had now attained the required steam pressure to roll, and the railroad man had become quite heated in his protests to Evans. He was doing a lot of arm waving and kept dangling a watch in front of Evans.

Railton had no sidewalks, even in front of the business premises. The whining wind and hiss of escaping steam covered the tread of Edge's boots as he approached the law office. Everyone at the depot was too busy to look along the street, and so failed to see the lean half-breed as he halted in the pale wedge of light that penetrated the glass panel of the office doorway. The sign angled out from the façade of the building read: *Abraham Barlow – Sheriff and Funeral Director.*

Edge rattled the handle as he opened the door, but the bald-headed man continued to sleep deeply in the leather armchair behind the desk. When Edge released the handle, the wind snatched the door away from him and banged it hard against the inside wall. The sheriff came awake with a snort as Edge stepped across the threshold. Dust from the street blew in around him. The dust made the lawman cough and the draught lifted the papers off his desk and scattered them.

'Shut the lousy door!' the sheriff yelled angrily, fisting the grit from his eyes with one hand while he tried to hold down papers with the other.

'Sure,' Edge answered, and did as he was asked.

The low-wicked lamp, hung from a hook in a ceiling beam, stopped swinging. The two men surveyed each other in its dim light. Barlow was about forty and looked like a man who had led a soft life. Pudgy, rather than out-and-out fat, with a round face the colour of dirty slush. He was dressed in pants and a long-sleeved, high-necked vest. A pot-bellied stove began to build up the temperature in the spartanly furnished office again. His dark eyes looked hard at Edge and his mouth adopted a line which suggested the man did not like what he saw.

'I sure as hell hope you're a guy called Edge,' he growled.

'Ain't such a bad night for you after all,' the half-breed told him, moving over to the stove and extending his hands towards it. He flexed his fingers, stiff from holding the reins in the cold air.

'What's left of it,' the lawman answered sourly. He reached behind him and took a Winchester from where it leaned against the wall. He rested it across the desk. Then he opened a drawer in the desk, took out a gunbelt with holstered Colt and put this atop the rifle. 'This ain't no lousy left luggage office, you know.'

'Take it up with the guy who left the stuff,' Edge told him, crossing to the desk.

Barlow shrugged his flabby shoulders. 'Ain't sayin' he didn't make it worth my while. But I'm a man who likes to sleep in a bed. Which is what I hope I can do soon as you leave.'

Edge had buckled the belt and tied the holster cord around his thigh. He took his time checking the load and action on the Colt. Even more time was used up in inspecting the Winchester. Then he nodded to the stony-faced lawman. 'Go to bed, sheriff,' he invited.

Barlow stood up. He wasn't very tall. About five feet six. He wasn't wearing a gunbelt. 'First like to be sure there's not goin' to be any trouble in my town.'

Edge pursed his lips. 'Going to be a killing, feller,' he said, turning to go to the door.

'Now, see here, mister!' Barlow snarled, whirling to reach behind him again.

But Edge had pivoted, too. And the Winchester was levelled and cocked before the lawman had curled his hand around his own rifle. 'Wear your sheriff's hat and there'll be two killings, feller,' the half-breed warned softly. 'Best you dust off the black stovepipe job, uh?'

Barlow gulped. 'I can't allow – '

'You were asleep. Won't be no one but the two of us know you woke up before they came to tell you there's a hole to dig.'

Edge lowered the Winchester and opened the door. Wind and dust blew in, but Barlow did not move. Not to hold down the skittering papers or to grab his rifle. The door closed and the shadowy form moved away from the glass panel. Then the sheriff dropped back into his chair and gulped again.

The self-willed bull had almost lost. His head and shoulders were inside the boxcar and a couple of long poles jabbed into his rump forced him all the way. Two men waiting at the sliding door shoved it across the gap. The railroad man glowered at Evans and ran across to the brake wagon to speak hurriedly with the brake man. Evans waved to his men, who were moving away from the side of the train to head for their horses which waited in one of the cattle pens. Evans walked fast towards the passenger car section of the train. The uniformed railroad man stepped back and the brake man sounded a bell and leaned out of the side of the wagon to swing a lamp. The locomotive whistle blasted and the train jerked forward.

A rifle shot cracked across the thud of pistons thrusting into cylinders.

The engineer and his fireman were intent upon moving their train. The brake man also decided that this was his prime concern. Everyone else stared in the direction from which the sound of the rifle shot came. Their shocked eyes saw the tall figure of Edge. He stood, with dust swirling around his legs and feet, at the point where the street opened up into the stockyard. The Winchester was held in his left hand, still aimed straight up into the night sky where the bullet had been fired. His right arm hung loosely at his side, hand level with the jutting butt of the holstered Colt.

The sound of the shot and the sight of the half-breed halted Evans in mid-stride. But the train was gaining speed.

'Take care of him!' he yelled, and lunged into a run, angling towards the rattling train. He only made it as far as the brake wagon. And he got no help from the brake man as he hauled himself up over the turning wheels. 'Kill the bum!' he screamed, his voice high and thin above the noise of the clattering train.

'Oh, my God!' the railroad man wailed, and turned to run towards the safety of the passenger depot.

Evans's nine men remained still, staring at the darkly clad man who only now lowered the Winchester, arcing it slightly to the side so that at no time was it aimed at the group. All the men had left their rifles in their saddle-boots. But, in the lamplight, Edge could see the butts of their revolvers jutting out from under the warm coats of the men on the fringe of the group.

'Ain't none of us gunfighters!' the rotund George Frimley whined.

It was easy to hear his words above the diminishing sound of the departing train and low wail of wind.

'Ain't but one of you I'm interested in,' Edge answered evenly. 'Unless you all figure I'm the same kind of easy pickings as Barnaby Tree.'

'Mr Evans ordered us to do that, mister!' the other fat man – Jeb – excused.

'And he ordered us to kill this guy!'

Edge recognised the voice of Brad, a mixture of anger and fear, coming from the centre of the cluster of men.

'I didn't hear him!' This from George Frimley, who scuttled away towards the horses in the pen.

'Me neither!' Clint agreed, and his skinny form moved fast after the fat one.

'I got no quarrel with you, mister!' Jeb said, as he hurried to make it a trio at the horses.

The other six remained where they were, looking across the low, moving dust at the lone figure of Edge. The half-breed stood immobile. But he was as ready to lunge into fast movement as he had been from the moment he squeezed the trigger to fire the warning shot. His hooded eyes were fixed upon the group. His right hand was poised to draw the Colt. Every muscle in his lean frame was coiled for the instant when he knew he would have to dive out of the way of a hail of bullets. The violent life that had aged his face beyond his years had keyed his reflexes to such a high pitch. First during the long years of the bloody War Between the States. Then in the harsh aftermath of that war. He had learned to respond instinctively to danger in order to survive. And to kill without compunction to preserve what was his. Yet he had lost everything but his life. Perhaps he had lost this, too, in the sense that violence had forged a different man from the ruin it had made of the former

Josiah C. Hedges. A man with the new name of Edge. But that was just a label. Many other changes had fashioned the tall figure who now stood at the dusty end of the single street in the rail-head town – prepared to gun down as many men as it needed to settle a grudge.

'One thing I need to know?' This from Hollis Millard, the man with the hare-lip.

Edge said nothing: waited and watched.

'You figure to get that bull?'

'Figure to get me a horse and the feller who took my guns is all.'

'I'm with them!' Millard growled, and made it four at the horses.

There was a short pause, and then a sudden burst of action as four men moved.

'Then there was one,' Edge muttered, but did not fix his attention rigidly on the lone figure of Brad standing in the open between the stock pens. He shot frequent glances towards the eight men formed into the new group.

Brad seemed not to trust himself to speak for long moments. Then he felt certain he could yell at the others without revealing his fear. 'You yellow bastards!' he accused.

'They made their move, feller,' Edge told him. 'Your turn to make yours.'

Brad swung his stare back towards Edge. 'A cowhand against a gunslinger?' he accused. His voice had a crack in it now. 'What kind of a fight is that, for God's sake?'

Edge did not reassess his opinion of the men who rode for Vic Evans. They were cowboys, not killers. The story Mathilda Tree had told him about the death of her brother simply meant that the men were cowboys who would kill if they had to. To keep their jobs – and maybe to help one of their number. He shook his head, glimpsing the huddle of men and looking longer at Brad's gun hand. 'For *my* sake, feller – one I aim to win.'

'First you gotta move it outside town limits, Edge!'

The voice of Sheriff Barlow snapped the order from behind and to the right of where the half-breed stood. All eyes except the cold blue ones shifted their surprised attention towards the law-man. They saw no one. Edge kept looking forward and knew precisely where Barlow was standing. In the recessed doorway of the stage depot which was the last building on that side of the street.

'Something wake you up?' Edge called.

'My lousy conscience, I figure. Or maybe my lousy sense of duty. Anyways, I ain't gonna have no gunfight in Railton.'

'You get a higher funeral fee for hauling a body across the town limits?' Edge taunted.

'You can't rile me,' Barlow growled. 'I got you covered, so don't make no lousy move unless it be outta town.'

Brad had been as surprised as the rest of Evans's men at the intervention of the sheriff. But, because it was his life that was on the line, he had recovered first. His stance had become tense and a certain eagerness had entered his steady eyes, pushing his fear into the background. Edge knew the man was set to make his move at the first clear chance he got. The half-breed offered him the chance.

'Object to having guns pointed at me, feller,' he said evenly, and started to turn. But only from the waist and, as his head swung, his eyes maintained their forward focus.

The wind moaned. Then came the rapid series of metallic clicks that were the sounds of Barlow's Winchester being pumped. The slow cadence of hooves at the walk and the creak of a heavily laden wagon in motion. Brad went for his gun.

'Don't!' one of Evans's men yelled.

The gun was fumbled clear of the holster and Brad showed a grin of triumph. He was a lot smoother cocking and levelling the revolver. But the grin broke up and became a look of nausea. For he knew he had been taken. Edge's lean body was like a statue and his head stayed half turned away. The Winchester, held low at its centre of balance, was pointed diagonally across the stockyard. But his right arm moved in a blur of speed, drawing, cocking and levelling the Frontier Colt.

Brad fired first because that was the way Edge wanted it. And now it was the rest of his body that moved while his right arm and hand remained rock steady. He leaned to the left and lunged down into a half crouch. Brad's bullet, fired from a gun in a trembling hand, went wide of the mark. Edge's Colt exploded a fraction of a second later. The bullet struck the target – the cowboy's chest, high up and left of centre. Brad died on his feet, with a cry of disappointment rather than pain. His arm dropped to his side and the gun slipped from his lifeless fingers. A small, dark stain on his sheepskin coat spread like a blossoming flower. The man's eyes stayed open. His mouth gaped wider. Then his head fell forward, his chin hitting his chest. The cold breeze gusted and helped gravity in knocking the dead body to the ground.

The wind moaned as the wagon was rolled to a creaking halt. Dust blew across the slumped form and some of it was trapped by the sticky wetness of the fresh blood. Edge drew himself erect and slid the Colt back into the holster. He faced his victim.

'Arresting or burying, sheriff?' the half-breed asked.

'Looked like self-defence to me,' the law-man growled.

'Can we leave?' Clint called.

'Without the dead man's horse,' Edge allowed.

'Sure thing,' another man agreed eagerly.

The pen gate was swung wide and the men crowded through. They mounted up fast and Hollis Millard led them out in a string, riding wide of where Brad grew stiff on the ground. George Frimley was last in the line, leading Evans's horse. A gelding remained in the pen. The men walked their horses around the rear of the passenger depot, then heeled them into a dust-billowing gallop along the side of the single track railroad.

'You know a name I can put on the lousy grave marker?' the law-man asked sourly as he stepped out of the doorway of the stage depot.

Edge turned around and noted that the sheriff had left his rifle behind him.

'It don't matter, mister!' Aunt Matty called. 'But his name was Bradford Bean.'

The reins were slapped across the backs of the team and the wagon jerked forward to roll down the final twenty yards of the street. Both women climbed down from the high seat and went to the rear of the wagon. Muriel Tree still limped on her sprained ankle. Barlow looked on in amazement as they took out two shovels and approached the body.

'What the lousy hell, ladies?' he roared. 'I take care of funerals in this town.'

'How much do you get for a burial, young feller?' Aunt Matty wanted to know, leaning on her shovel.

Edge moved over to the pen holding the single horse. He took the Winchester from the boot, dropped it to the ground and replaced it with his own. Then he started to check over the horse, saddle and bedroll. He nodded his approval, but began to uncinch the saddle.

'Anything from five bucks to fifty, depending on how special.'

Aunt Matty dug out a five dollar bill from a pocket of her long coat, screwed it up and tossed it towards the surprised law-man. 'This skunk don't want nothin' special. And me and Mu'll make sure that's what he gets.'

Barlow caught the bill as it blew on the wind with the expertise of a man with a knack for acquiring easy money. 'Well, I'll be . . . ' he said with a shrug.

Edge had dropped Brad's saddle to the ground and led the horse from the pen. 'Don't point a gun at me again and you'll carry on being,' he said flatly as he steered the horse towards the rear of the wagon.

He reached over the tail-gate and took out his own saddle. Then he continued to lead the horse back along the street, heading for the hotel he had passed on his first walk through the town. It was easier to see this time, because the two shots had roused the local citizenry. Lighted windows squared the formerly dark façades of most of the buildings, and the heads and shoulders of the curious were silhouetted against them. Back at the stockyard, the sheriff watched in awe as the two women lifted the body of the dead man and carried him out on to waste ground beyond the pens.

'Hey mister!' a voice croaked from a partially open doorway

as Edge ambled by. 'What's happenin'? Who's that the women are haulin'?'

'Kinda like Santa Claus on Christmas Eve,' the half-breed answered cryptically as he angled towards the hotel entrance.

'How's that?' the puzzled watcher asked.

'He's Bean. Now he's gone.'

# Chapter Four

EDGE shaved, bathed and slept after ensuring that the hotel livery took care of his newly acquired piebald gelding. He paid in advance for his room and the stabling service. Thus, when he rose and left the hotel at daybreak, there was no reason to wake anybody else. But he was not the only man awake in Railton as he set off at a walking pace astride his horse heading south down the street, shaded from the first rays of sunlight by the buildings on his left. For, as he emerged into the stockyard, he saw a figure over beyond the pens. He reined his horse around in that direction and recognised the uniformed railroad man who had been in such a hurry last night.

The man was standing at one end of a low, narrow mound of freshly dug earth. At the other end, a small headstone had been set up. The railroad man did a double-take at Edge, recognised him, and became nervous.

'Morning,' Edge said easily.

The man blinked, licked his lips and recovered his composure. He took off his peaked cap to scratch his head and nodded towards the small, marble tombstone. 'Ain't that the queerest thing you ever did see?' he asked.

Edge cracked his eyes against the sunlight shafting through the clear, still air of morning. 'Plain you never did meet a feller named Bob Rhett,' he answered, drawing a quizzical look from Railton's other early riser. He heeled his horse into a position where he could read the carefully inscribed, black-stained lettering on the grey of the stone: DEAD FROM MURDERING BARNABY TREE. 'The local mason cuts a neat stone,' he said.

The railroad man replaced his cap and shook his head. 'Them women had the marker in the back of their wagon. Already had the letterin' on it. Watched 'em myself set the stone on the mound after they filled in the grave.'

Edge nodded and looked down at the ground around the stockyard. 'Figured the wagon was riding a little heavy for a rig loaded with just hay,' he muttered.

But now there were just the footprints of the railroad man and the hoof tracks of the gelding in the dust. The wind which had now subsided had covered whatever sign had been made last night.

'Headed south at the side of the railroad,' the man supplied. 'Old lady in the back and the young one drivin'. Asked me where the guy and the bull was booked through to. Told 'em Dry Lake Bend. That's where the tracks stop goin' south and swing to the west.'

Edge took out the makings and rolled a cigarette. 'Should I be interested, feller?' he wanted to know evenly.

The man shrugged. 'They said that if you asked, I was to tell you. You didn't ask, but I told you anyway.' He squinted up at the tall man lighting the cigarette. 'Anythin' wrong with that?'

Edge flipped the dead match down on to the grave. 'Nothing, feller,' he agreed, raised a hand in farewell and heeled the gelding forward.

'Sure glad about that!' the railroad man called after him.

'Like to spread a little happiness,' the half-breed tossed in reply, angling his horse to go around the back of the passenger depot. Then he set the gelding on a straight course, due south along the side of the sun-glinting rails. Ahead, the track disappeared into the heat shimmer and soon, the morning haze to the north drew an ethereal veil across the town of Railton.

The ground began to slope downwards and the heat began to build up. At noon, he rested in the shade of a water-tower at the side of the track after allowing the gelding to drink from the hose. He ate some jerked beef and sour-dough bread and contemplated a share of fifty thousand dollars. The thoughts aided his digestion and when he climbed into the saddle after the break, he demanded more speed from his horse.

At mid-afternoon he saw the first sign left by those who had taken this route before him. He was at a place that had been sheltered from the wind of the previous night. The ground was sandy here and held the impressions of many hoof prints, over-scored by the parallel ruts of a laden wagon. The sign made no difference to Edge. There had probably been others during the morning – discarded cigarette butts, horse-droppings and patches of dried wet – which he had failed to see because he was not looking for them. But the clearly visible railroad track pointed the way to Dry Lake Bend.

When he reached this point, the sun was red heralding evening and he guessed he had lost perhaps three thousand feet of altitude. There was still a lot of residual heat from the afternoon and the night would probably be a lot warmer than it had been up in the higher country. The Dry Lake was a big one – an enormous dish of cracked ground to the east of a range of low hills. The railroad made a wide sweep around the eastern shore and the station was at midway point. It was not much of a place. There was a water-tower, a high stack of cut logs and a shack. On the side of the tank on top of the tower was a sign which proclaimed the name of the station. The Tree's wagon was parked outside the shack and the team had been unhitched. The four stallions were drinking water from a trough beneath the tower as Aunt Matty pumped a fresh supply into it.

Edge, a cigarette hung from the corner of his mouth, walked his horse over the final hundred yards to Dry Lake Bend. And the woman did not hear the clop of hooves until the man and animal were crossing the top of the long shadow from the tower. Then she snapped her head around from staring at the shack. She had not been concentrating on her chore and the water was brimming over the lip of the trough. There was a familiar expression of hatred on her ugly face, but it was not directed at the half-breed. Relief showed briefly when she recognised the newcomer. Then she stopped pumping and made to run towards him.

But a scream exploded from inside the shack. A man laughed.

'Come here and do like I say, you bitch!' the man yelled.

The woman screamed again and footfalls thudded on a hollow floor. The door was wrenched open and Muriel Tree lunged out into the evening sunlight. It glowed on her sweat-sheened nakedness, glinting on the beads that coursed across her quivering flesh – over her big, bouncing breasts; around the slight bulge of her trembling belly; and down her well-formed, pumping thighs. The terrified woman pulled up short and stared blindly around her, wiping the tears from her eyes. Then she saw Aunt Matty and plunged towards the older woman.

Edge halted his horse at the end of the trough and the gelding dipped his head to drink. Across the backs of the other drinking animals, the half-breed grimaced at what had been done to the beautiful body of Muriel Tree. From neck to midway down her thighs, she had been assaulted by a ravaging mouth. Dull red teeth marks showed against the milk-white flesh. Here and there among the forming bruises were trickles of dried blood. She flung herself into the arms of the older woman, not seeing Edge through her terror. A terror that heightened still more as a naked man lumbered out of the shack, bellowing like a crazed Indian on the warpath. He pulled up short and glowered around him, blinking against the rays of the dying sun. Muriel screamed and tore out of Aunt Matty's embrace to cower behind the more slightly built woman. The sound drew the man's lustful attention to where his quarry was seeking refuge.

'We struck a bargain, you bitches!' he snarled, swinging around and starting to amble like a grizzly bear towards the water trough.

He looked something like a grizzly: at least six feet tall, and solidly built to a weight of more than two hundred and fifty pounds. Most of his bulk seemed to be hard-packed flesh with plenty of muscle. But, despite his nakedness, there was not a lot of flesh to be seen, for he carried a thick matting of black hair. Only his feet and the palms of his hands were free of it. And on his head, just his brow and cheeks, for he wore a thick beard. Another heavy mane grew from his skull. Edge guessed he was on the downward slide out of middle-age.

Suddenly, he glimpsed Edge astride the drinking horse and he pulled up short. The way his eyes were glazed and his hirsute body swayed, the half-breed guessed the man was drunk with something more substantial than sex.

'What the friggin' hell are you doin' here?' the big man demanded.

Aunt Matty and Muriel snapped their heads around. The older woman's eyes pleaded for help. If Muriel recognised the half-breed, she saw him only as another man. She gaped her mouth for a scream but her vocal chords seized up.

'Thinking, feller.'

'Thinkin' what?'

Edge curled back his lips to show a cold, thin grin. 'That I don't reckon mine much.'

'Please!' the older woman begged. 'Our horses were droppin'. They had to have water. He said Muriel had to pay for it.'

Edge raked his eyes from the ugly face of Aunt Matty to the despoiled body of Muriel. 'Water comes high in these parts. Hope my mount don't drink that much.'

'Water him and get on your way, mister!' the naked man ordered. 'This here's railroad property and you're trespassin'.'

He took another unsteady step. Muriel clung to Aunt Matty, who continued to stare at Edge in desperation. Then a knowing look entered her eyes.

'We'll pay you, Edge!' she rasped.

'Ain't interested in the fortune you two ladies are sitting on. Third of that high priced beefsteak on legs'll do.'

Aunt Matty didn't have to think about it. 'You're on!' she snapped.

'Lucky for the horses she ain't,' Edge replied as he nodded at Muriel and jerked on the reins to raise the gelding's head and steer him around the team.

'Beat it, I told you!' the hairy man snarled, standing his ground as the mounted half-breed approached. 'Don't you mess with me, mister. One time I took four bullets and then killed the bastard with my bare hands.'

Edge's hooded eyes raked over the man at close quarters and he believed that the warning was no idle boast. Little less than both loads in a double-barrelled shotgun could be guaranteed to drop a man like this at a first attempt. He halted the horse a couple of feet in front and slightly to the side of the hirsute giant. 'Seems to me the lady paid what she owes for the water, feller.' He tried a man-to-man leer. 'With plenty of interest.'

'I'll say when she's paid!' His eyes had cleared of their glaze now. There was no longer a slur in his voice. But the liquor still had a grip on his sense of balance and he swayed as if in a gentle evening breeze.

Edge sighed. 'I don't want to have to kill you, feller,' he said softly.

The giant laughed – longer and louder than in the shack. He cupped his palms over his hips and threw back his head. The hair on his head, face and body glistened in the sunlight as he quivered with mirth. Edge sat watching and waiting, apparently at ease and off-guard. But, recalling his attitude during the gunfight at Railton, Aunt Matty knew the pose was a lie.

'Go and get dressed, Muriel,' she whispered to her sister-in-law. 'It's all over now.'

But Muriel, withdrawing back from the brink of hysteria, was still gripped by a fear that froze the sweat on her naked, assaulted body. She did not hear the words of Aunt Matty and maintained her wide-eyed stare at the two men. When the naked man, still laughing, lunged at the mounted half-breed, she vented a shrill moan of defeat.

The attack he had been expecting triggered Edge into instant action. Not fast, but deliberate. He slid his feet from the stirrups and leaned forward, into the hairy embrace of the giant's curving arms. But he held his own arms out from his sides, bent slightly at the elbows. As he was dragged out of the saddle, his captor curtailed the laughter and vented a murderous roar that gusted foul-smelling breath into Edge's face. The horse snorted and veered away in fright at the new sound.

While the half-breed was in mid-air, held tight against the naked front of the man by a crushing grip, he timed two moves simultaneously. One was to lash a kick between the splayed legs of the giant. The second was to straighten his arms. It was the front of his calf that crashed into the crotch of the man. Not as hard as his boot would have been: but hard enough to wrench a groan of pain and momentarily weaken the victim. The weakness lasted just long enough for the man not to be able to counteract the arm-straightening tactic. And, when he did try to reassert his crushing embrace, the half-breed had slipped through the trap to crouch on the ground.

Edge snapped into higher speed now, streaking his left hand to the nape of his neck. The giant bent down to claw at his shoulders, digging in his powerful fingers and wrenching upwards. The action aided his opponent. Edge's left hand aimed for the man's stomach, wrist turning to swivel the blade of the razor. The upward momentum into which he was forced did the rest. The blade sank half its length into the pulpy flesh above the giant's legs. Warm moisture gushed out over Edge's hand. The giant did not begin to scream until the blade started a slicing action. It found a more resistant target and its wielder had to use his own strength as the double grip on his shoulders was released. The big man fell backwards, clawing for the source of his agony. The blade came free as blood started to pour from the wound.

The touch of hands increased the man's pain and he flung his arms wide as he fell to his knees. Blood and less vividly coloured liquid drained from the terrible wound and was eagerly soaked up by the ground. The man's scream subsided to a moan and he fell into a faint.

The half-breed swung around and strode to the water-trough. The horses had drunk their fill, and he had to pump out some more from the tank on top of the tower. He held his hand and the razor under the hose as the two women watched him. Neither of them seemed to trust herself to speak.

'She can get dressed and you can hitch the wagon now,' the half-breed told Aunt Matty evenly. 'He won't be bothering you ladies any more.'

'Nor nobody else for sure after that,' the older woman replied hoarsely.

'Charged too much for the water, ma'am. Couldn't give back what he took. Have to be content with splitting the difference.'

The disablement of her assaulter and the easy tones in which Edge spoke had the effect of calming Muriel Tree, and she emerged from her torment aware that the cool blue eyes were surveying her body. She emitted a squeal – of violated modesty – and sprinted for the open doorway of the shack, curving wide of the sprawled form on the ground.

'Muriel and me are real grateful to you, mister,' Aunt Matty said as she gathered up the trailing traces and urged the team over to the front of the wagon.

'Third of fifty grand grateful, way I hear it,' the half-breed answered. He also went over to the wagon, but towards the rear.

'You hear right,' Aunt Matty admitted openly. 'You'll be ridin' with us, I guess?'

He hauled himself up over the tail-gate and moved some bales of hay. He found a wooden crate with a hinged lid and looked inside. It contained grave markers that were identical to the one which was on the mound above the body of Bradford Bean back at Railton. He counted them. Nine. Then he dropped the lid back on the crate, replaced the hay bales and dropped down to the ground. He checked that his horse had not wandered far, and then rolled a cigarette as he watched the woman hitch the team.

'I'll be with you, ma'am,' he told her. 'But just to protect my investment. You do the other nine killings yourself.'

She continued with her chores, doing it like an expert. 'My

third husband was a stonemason. I learned the trade from him.'

Edge blew out smoke. 'Which number was the killer?'

Aunt Matty tested the tension of the traces, nodded her satisfaction and sighed. She climbed up on to the seat. Weariness gave her face a haggard look that accentuated nature's unkindness to her features.

'Never did finish telling you the story of that bull, did I, young feller?' She sniffed. 'After Vic Evans and his hands got off scot-free for murdering Barnaby, Muriel had this strong urge to kill them all at the first chance she got. But I wasn't for that – couldn't see how a slip of a girl like that could do it. But I made up those tombstones to humour her, kind of. Took a long time over it, hoping her crazy anger would cool. It did, some. Changed her mind. Said she wanted to get the bull and bring him down to Texas. Intention was to get the money and use it to hire the best lawyers and force a trial for the killers.'

'Markers just for ballast in the high winds?' the half-breed suggested wryly.

'Who's tellin' the damn story?' Aunt Matty demanded angrily.

'You don't get golden spurs for length, ma'am.'

She ignored him. 'I told Muriel I'd go for that. I helped her get the bull out of the Evans spread and I've been with her on the long haul down here. I almost quit when I found she'd put the tombstones aboard, but we was down south of Oregon territory by then and a long way from home. To boot, there was no sign that the Evans bunch were tracking us. Until the other night, which you know about.'

'Changed you some, uh?'

The familiar expression of hatred re-entered the woman's face. 'Changed me a lot, young feller,' she said venomously. 'Now I'm all for using every one of them tombstones.' A sniff. 'But I ain't so sure about Muriel. I don't know if she's got the gall to kill a man.'

The object of the woman's doubt emerged from the shack, dressed in a long gown that didn't cover everything it was supposed to. In the heat of his lust, the giant had ripped off one sleeve at the shoulder, popped several buttons below the high neckline and torn a long rent at the thigh. On her face, Muriel wore a vague expression of one in deep thought. But there was nothing vague about her stride as she walked towards the unconscious man with the blood-drenched groin. She had a gunbelt strapped around her waist, with a full load of shells and the butt of a Remington .44 jutting from the holster. She held a wooden box in one hand and in the other carried a single-barrelled hammerless shotgun with a lot of fancy decoration on the hinged frame.

'That gets us out of a bind,' Aunt Matty said softly, calling Edge's attention to her face, which was now expressing tight-lipped pleasure. 'Evans's men kept our guns,' she amplified. 'And that bastard of a sheriff back in Railton wouldn't allow us to buy any new ones in town. Figured I'd have to ask you for a loan of yours, which you wouldn't have agreed to, right?'

Edge dropped the cigarette and trod it into the ground. 'Not in a million years, ma'am,' he answered, and moved to retrieve his horse.

'And we ain't got nowhere near that much time,' Aunt Matty said, picking up the reins. 'Come on, Mu, we got to be mov . . . '

Her voice trailed away as the half-breed swung up into the saddle. Both of them looked towards Muriel, who had halted at the side of the wounded man.

'Leave him to die, my dear!' the older woman muttered brutally. 'He deserves it.'

Muriel stared down at her assaulter, her blonde hair sweeping in front of her face to hide her expression. 'A train might come, Mathilda.'

'Then he'll suffer worse – a man like him – if he lives.'

The golden hair trembled as Muriel shook her head. 'But I won't have made him pay for what he did to me. Terrible things, Mathilda. I'll get sick just thinking about them. And then, after he did all that, do you know what he wanted me to do?'

'I've been married five times, Muriel,' Aunt Matty replied

dully. 'Ain't nothing I don't know about what men like to do to women.'

Muriel placed the box on the ground as her sister-in-law was speaking. She opened the lid, took out a cartridge, slid it into the breech and snapped the gun closed.

'She's kind of young,' Edge called softly, watching Muriel as she stood up and took aim with the shotgun. 'But looks like she's going through the change, ma'am.'

'He wanted me to take him in my mouth!' Muriel said shrilly, lowered the gun and squeezed the trigger.

The recoil thrust the woman backwards, and took her out of range of the gushing gore. The shot pellets smashed into the bearded face between his upper lip and his flared nostrils. They spread inside his mouth and tore through flesh, gristle and bone until they buried themselves in the ground beneath. The entire top three-quarters of the man's head disintegrated in a crimson and white explosion of blood and bone fragments. His body did not move. Both his eyes survived whole, and floated away from him on a river of blood. They stared accusingly up at the sky as it darkened in the wake of the setting sun. Another moving river was formed: from a different direction and coloured black. A column of ants was marching in for an unexpected feast.

'Live ones won't be so easy,' Edge warned, watching the woman closely for a hysterical response to the ghastly result of her action.

But she was calm and deliberate as she returned to the side of the mutilated man and picked up the box of shotgun cartridges. She stepped demurely over the inert form and moved to the wagon. She no longer limped.

'He got what he deserved!' she said emphatically as she climbed aboard and sat down hard on the seat.

'Even what he wanted,' Edge growled, eyeing the corpse, messily decapitated above the mouthline. He spat as he wheeled his horse. 'A little head.'

# Chapter Five

A MOON – fuller, higher and brighter than last night – made tracking easy. Even more helpful was the trackers' knowledge of their quarry's ultimate destination. But, for the first few miles east of Dry Lake Bend, Edge rode ahead of the wagon to assure himelf that Evans and his men really were making in the general direction of distant El Paso.

Then he dropped back, hitched the gelding to the tail-gate and ran forward to haul himself up on to the seat of the moving wagon. Muriel Tree had the reins now, while Aunt Matty vented regular snorting sounds from inside the covered wagon.

'We take it in turns,' the woman explained. 'One sleeps while the other one drives. We think that, even with the bull, Evans can move faster than a wagon.'

The half-breed was experiencing a weariness of his own after the long ride under the hot sun. 'Sounds like a great idea,' he said, his tone suggesting it was not. 'If you can be sure of picking up a new team of horses every once in a while.'

Muriel continued to stare straight ahead, but her profile became set in hard lines. 'We aren't stupid, Mr Edge! We did bring this rig all the way down from the Canadian border, you know, and with the same team!'

The reason she had to keep her attention to the front was

that the leading pair tended to veer from side to side. The pair behind were equally as tired, ready to go meekly where the others led.

'We stop for one hour at the end of every four,' she added.

'Ain't enough,' the half-breed warned. 'Figure the team had longer than an hour at the last stop and they ain't been hauling more than thirty minutes since. Yet they're close to dropping in their tracks, ma'am.'

'Attend to your own business, mister, and I'll attend to mine,' Muriel snapped. 'You saw what I did back there to get the animals water. Doesn't that show I've got the team's interest at heart?'

'Shows you're anxious to catch up with the bull,' Edge answered. He leaned across and snatched the reins out of her hands.

Muriel gave a cry of angry surprise and whirled in the seat to glare at the half-breed. 'What do you think you're doing?' she demanded.

'Over anxious, I'd say,' he replied steering the team down a slight slope to the left and easing them to a halt on a patch of tough grass to one side of a grove of mixed mesquite and cactus plants.

'What's all the ruckus?' Aunt Matty demanded sleepily from the rear.

'This . . . this . . . man is making us stop, Mathilda!' Muriel stuttered in anger.

Edge hitched the reins around the brake lever and jumped down to the ground. He started to release the team from their traces. 'We're in the same business, Mrs Tree,' he told the woman who sat in rigid anger on the seat. 'Which means we'll both fail if the horses don't hold out.'

'Not *both*, young feller,' Aunt Matty put in as she came along the side of the wagon. 'This is a three-handed operation. And I'm glad you got the point across to Mu.' She glowered up at the younger woman. 'I been tellin' her all along we been pushing the animals too hard.'

Muriel shared her glare of frustrated anger between Aunt Matty and Edge. Then she pouted. 'We've got to get to a town soon where we can change the team!' she maintained. 'The longer we stop, the farther Evans will get in front of us.'

'Evans and his men have got horses, too,' Edge pointed out, continuing with the chore of unhitching the team. 'And the bull. Men and animals alike have got to rest and to eat.'

Aunt Matty sniffed. 'Told her all that.'

'Actions speak louder than words,' the half-breed answered, freeing the team and then ground-hobbling them.

'Tried it, young feller,' Aunt Matty said, with a stern glance at Muriel. 'But she's younger and stronger than me. Real strong when she's in a temper.'

Edge was on his way to attend to his own horse at the rear of the wagon. 'Figure she's a little younger than me. But I can take care of her in the other department.'

He was out of sight of Muriel, but she flinched at the sound of his fist smacking into an open palm. Then she got a defiant look into her green eyes as she draped a hand over the Remington in her holster. She stared down at Aunt Matty, and her mouth took on the line of a sneer. 'You try to lay a finger on me, mister, and you'll regret it, I'm telling you.'

Aunt Matty grinned along the side of the wagon at Edge, who was unsaddling the gelding. 'And that skunk Evans called *me* a tough egg,' she rasped.

Edge responded to the grin with one of his own. 'I know which one I'd like to go to work on,' he said wryly.

After that, he lit a fire and his chores were over for the night. Whistling, Aunt Matty prepared a meal while the sullen-faced Muriel spread fodder for the horses and watered them. While they ate, the younger woman maintained a stony silence, and her older sister-in-law chattered about inconsequentials for a short time. Edge was tired and the food hastened his weariness towards a point where he was ready for sleep.

'It wasn't a third of what the bull fetches we intended to offer you,' Aunt Matty said. She had been talking about her husbands, explaining that her fifth and last had been called D'Eath, which was why she had reverted to her maiden name. Edge had been listening to the sound of her voice, rather than the words. Even though it was obvious Aunt Matty was talking to him rather than the sulking Muriel. But this sudden change of subject snapped him out of his dozing state.

'Got your message from the railroad man,' he said from under his hat, tipped forward over his face as his head rested on his bedroll..

'Sorry we told him what we did,' Muriel put in coldly. 'We can handle this business ourselves.'

Aunt Matty sniffed. 'Maybe we can and maybe we can't. But back at Railton weren't neither of us so full of spunk.' She looked at the lounging Edge and moderated her tone. 'Figured to offer you fifty dollars a day to ride escort for us. On account of there being Indian country up ahead.'

'Deal's made, ma'am,' the half-breed said.

'I know it,' was the quick reply. 'Just wanted you to be aware – '

'I think we made the best deal,' Muriel interrupted acidly. 'Man like he is, he'd have taken us to Texas by way of Philadelphia and got enough days' work to get every cent we're going to make.'

Edge raised his head and tilted back his hat so he could send a cold stare at the younger woman. She saw the harshness in those eyes, and the cruel line of the thin mouth made her catch her breath. His voice seemed to extract every trace of warmth from around the glowing fire.

'Mrs Tree, something you ought to know. Night ain't long enough to tell you all the things I'm not. One of the few things I am is honest. You make any more accusations like that and I'll kill you. That's a promise.'

He tilted his hat forward again and rested his head back on the bedroll. Muriel grew scarlet as she let out her pent-up breath. Then she sucked in another and seemed on the point of hurling an angry retort at the half-breed.

'Talk of money's premature anyways!' Aunt Matty put in hurriedly. 'First, catch the bull.'

'Thank you, Mrs Beaton,' Edge muttered sleepily from under his hat.

'You *were* listening!' Aunt Matty said gleefully. 'Mr Beaton was my third.'

'Cook, was he?'

'No, that was Grayson Kerr, my second. Beaton wrote books. I told you that.'

'Long ones?' Edge's voice was little more than a whisper now.

'Very long,' Aunt Mattty answered. 'There was one time he was working on this . . . '

Edge thought he said: 'You sure did learn something from all your husbands, ma'am.' But, although the comment was formed in his mind, he did not speak it. He was asleep too soon.

As it always had been from those first few days after the initial action of the War Between the States, the kind of sleep Edge took was refreshing, but light. Even when there was no imminent threat of danger, his mind sank to only a shallow plane of unconsciousness and a highly developed sixth sense remained alert. Thus, he slumbered undisturbed through the sounds the women made in clearing away the remains of the meal and bedding down in their tent. But, had a twig cracked in the wrong place, or a horse other than the five at the campsite given a low snort, the half-breed would have woken instantly prepared to respond like lightning to whatever menace lurked in the shadows beyond the glow of the fire.

In fact, it was the first ray of a new day's sun that nudged him into an easy waking. There was not a cloud in sight in the clear blue sky and the seemingly limitless landscape of scrub desert showed no sign of being host to any other intruders than those who were camped beside the grove. He boiled water for shaving and coffee, then roused the women. This took some effort, revealing just how exhausted they had been. He finally had to resort to prodding the muzzle of his Winchester into a bulge at one side of the tent.

'Hey, careful where you're poking that thing!' Muriel snarled.

'Only my gun, ma'am,' Edge said lightly.

'Go to hell!'

'Guess that's gotta be where I'm headed in the end,' he replied ruefully.

*

They made steady progress all through that day, across the desert and up into high country again. They often saw signs left by the group of men they were following. Aunt Matty did a lot of talking during the morning, but her mood became less buoyant during the afternoon. On occasions when she thought that the other two were not looking at her, she allowed a grimace of pain to carve deeper lines into her face. Sleeping on the ground with only canvas to keep out the night air was not good for her rheumatism. But she was determined that Muriel and Edge should not be aware of her suffering. Muriel spoke only when it was strictly necessary. Edge was his taciturn self, dividing his time between riding on the wagon and taking his gelding ahead to scout for a sign or find the easiest way around natural obstacles.

He did spot the older woman's discomfort, but it was not in his nature to interfere in affairs that did not concern him. Only if Aunt Matty's disability hampered efforts to win back the bull would she become a problem. Although he ignored Muriel Tree's vexation to the same extent, he did detect a certain change in her attitude. He guessed that now he was merely a current excuse to provide a handy reason for her mood. Maybe the real motive for her pouting sourness was in the past. Was it what the man at Dry Lake Bend had done to her, or what she had done to him?

He didn't give a damn and, after a while, he ceased to think about her as a means of filling the long hours under the hot sun. And, a little later, he admitted to himself just why, in truth, he had forced the woman out of his mind. That he didn't give a damn was only part of the reason. The major share was because, in thinking about Muriel Tree, he kept conjuring up a mental image of her naked. And not an image of the reality he had seen at the railroad watering stop. Instead, a vivid imaginary picture of the naked body without the marks of her assaulter's savagery.

Like honesty, a strong sexual drive was one of the few other facets of a man which had survived the dehumanising effects of an evil war and a cruel peace. But, unlike honesty, there was a time and a place to indulge lust. And neither condition existed out here in the wilderness.

He called a halt early, when there was still plenty of light left, and neither woman made any objection. Aunt Matty was obviously relieved that her aged bones and stiffened joints were to be given a break from the jolting and bouncing of the wagon. Muriel seemed to have withdrawn into a private world in which she had become little more than an automaton: she needed to be told what to do, and she did it silently and absently.

But when, after they had eaten, Edge explained what he had in mind, the younger woman responded with an eager smile that held more than a touch of evil.

'It's about time we did something,' she rasped, and caressed the butt of the Remington. 'Today it's been like we were out on a Sunday picnic ride.'

'Had you figured wrong, young feller,' Aunt Matty said without enthusiasm. 'Reckoned you intended for Evans and his men to have the trouble of that bull until we was almost at journey's end.'

Edge nodded and lit a cigarette. 'Thought about it, ma'am. But journey's end is a long way off. And, like you pointed out, we've got to cross Apacheria to get there. I'll ride easier knowing I'm taking care of my own investment.'

They bedded down before the sun slipped from sight behind the western mountain range, and rose many hours before it was due to make a reappearance in the east. The two periods of rest with the easy travel in between had eased the strain on the women and they woke with less trouble this time. With a full day's supplies in his saddle-bags and both canteens filled with water, Edge galloped the gelding into the darkness of the early hours while Aunt Matty and Muriel were still breaking camp.

He didn't think he would need the supplies, for the signs he had seen during the previous day's ride looked quite fresh. Whether from confidence they were not being followed or another reason, Evans and his men were not setting a fast pace. Edge rode as hard as was possible without exhausting the gelding, and stopped often, but not to rest. Instead he was marking his trail with short lengths of brightly coloured thread which he had taken from Aunt Matty's work-basket.

He had been travelling for about two and a half hours when he saw the glow of a fire ahead. It was no more than a faint tinge of orange that formed an aura above the crest of a humped hill, about two miles away when he first saw it. He kept the gelding to a gallop over the first mile, then halted and dumped a whole bundle of threads on the ground. He walked the horse over the final stretch, and along a broad gully that emerged at the base of the hill.

He hitched the reins around a branch of mesquite and slid the Winchester from the saddle-boot as he dismounted. He gave the horse a drink from his hat and then started to climb the hill. It was steep and rocky on this side, but there were adequate hand and footholds and he reached the hundred and fifty feet high crest in less than thirty minutes. He glanced back over the moonlit landscape of rocks and sparse vegetation but failed to see any trace of the Trees' wagon.

Turning back, he went down on his stomach and squirmed his way up and over the smooth hump of the hill crest. On the south side, the hill fell away in a gentle slope for perhaps a quarter of a mile. At the base was a sheltered oasis: a flat area of tough grass with a small stream running across it. The stream appeared from a hole in the base of a low cliff on the right, flowed smoothly across the level area and became noisy and white as it entered an expanse of grotesquely shaped rocks on the left. A half mile beyond where the hillside levelled out, there were two more high cliffs, split at the centre by the mouth of a canyon.

The fire was on the bank of the stream, midway between where it made its appearance and where it rushed into the forest of rocky pinnacles. The men slept in a half circle to one side of the fire. Edge counted nine elongated humps, which meant no one was standing guard. The horses were ground-hobbled twenty yards from the fire, on the low cliff side. The bull, tied to a stake driven into the ground and with its back legs shackled by an iron chain, was on the same side of the fire, but a lot farther away – immediately under the cliff.

Having studied all this for a few seconds, Edge looked elsewhere. First eastwards, but as yet there was not the faintest trace of the grey of dawn to relieve the star-pricked darkness of night on the skyline. Then, for longer, he peered into the north. And was rewarded with the sight of a single dot of black that moved among the larger, immobile areas of darkness on darkness. The women were at least two miles away, but closing with every second that passed.

He checked that the men below were still soundly asleep, and started to move to his right, still on his belly. The hump of the hill, polished smooth by a million years of weather, began to slope downwards. But not all the way to the level of the night camp. It merged with the face of the low cliff and became a sheer drop itself, directly opposite where the horses were hobbled. It was a drop of thirty feet, and Edge cursed as he peered over the rim and failed to see any holes or ledges.

A horse raised his head, froze, and then whinnied. The others caught Edge's scent and joined in raising the alarm. The bull also looked around with a baleful eye but kept his peace.

'Mr Evans!' A harsh whisper.

Edge pressed himself against the ground after pulling back from the rim.

'What the friggin' hell, Clint?' a man groaned.

'Tell Mr Evans somethin's stirred the horses. And keep your lousy voice down!'

The man lowered his voice, but his tone remained just as disgruntled as before. 'So go check on it, mulehead. You wanna wake everyone to go lookin' for a gopher or somethin'?'

Edge could see the men at the camp-fire clearly. Two of them were sitting up while the others continued breathing heavily or snoring. Then one of them slammed down flat again with a noisy sigh. The second remained sitting upright, body rigid and head swinging slowly from side to side. The horses by now had accepted Edge's presence, and had calmed down. Then a coyote howled in the far distance and the horses shuffled and snorted again.

'Yellow nags!' Clint snarled as he lay down.

'Brave as you, mulehead!' the other man muttered sleepily.

Edge counted the seconds until two minutes had passed and

then started back up the slope. When he reached the top, he froze. Nothing visible moved against the northern panorama now, but he could hear the beat of hooves – subdued, but distinctly audible. He snatched a look down at the camp and vented a low grunt of satisfaction. The bulk of the hill would effectively stop the sound from reaching the ears of the sleeping men.

But he couldn't risk taking the easy way down the gentle slope. It would just need a loose pebble rolling to rouse Evans and his hands and they would spot the intruder immediately on the exposed hillside.

So he started down the slope on the opposite side to the first one he had tried. This time he got lucky. The decline was steeper and rougher, but it went all the way down to the level he wanted and petered out at the edge of the cluster of rocks. He could walk upright over the final few yards. And back-tracking towards the camp-site, he could make a noise without attracting attention, for the rushing white water of the stream acted as a cover.

Time was running out, for either the arrival of dawn or the appearance of the women could ruin the part of the plan he had not told Aunt Matty and Muriel about. As far as they knew, he intended to trap Evans and his men and hold them prisoner, to be put at the mercy of the women. He had not said this in so many words, but the women had inferred it. Muriel had gleefully expressed what her intentions would be in such a situation.

But it was the bull that Edge was after. The men who had stolen it were not his concern because they had not heisted it from him.

At the edge of the rocks, he turned off the direct route to the camp-site, swinging wide to go around it from the south. Halfway round, far from cover, he glanced over his shoulder and quickened his pace. A faint, but clearly perceptible lightening of the sky was visible above the cluster of rocks. The ground underfoot was hard and he didn't risk running. He merely lengthened the stride of his rangy legs, setting his boots down cautiously as though he were walking on broken glass.

He reached the shadows at the base of the low cliff and moved in on his objective. The shadows would not last for long. The eastern sky was now a definite grey colour which was advancing to lighten the entire dome of the heavens. Mucus dripped from the flared nostrils of the bull who winked a dark eye at the man who drew near to him. The horses shuffled and tugged at their tethers, impatient to start another day's work. The men at the side of the fire breathed regularly or snored and grunted. Edge inched around to the back of the bull. The animal turned his head, eyes no longer blinking. He swished his tail and pawed at the ground with a forehoof.

'Bastard!' the half-breed breathed. Then, the harshness gone from his tone, he matched the baleful look in the animal's eyes. 'Not you, feller.'

The shackles were fancy ones. A length of stout chain about eighteen inches long, with a ring at each end which were snapped around the animal's hindlegs. Snapped, and fixed securely in position with a padlock on each. There was no way to move the bull unless the padlocks were unfastened to free the rings.

Edge backed away from the rear of the bull so that he was able to look round the group of horses at the sleeping men. It didn't need the firelight to illuminate them now. Dawn had broken. With their boss present, the half-breed wasn't prepared to risk trying to cover them all with a single gun while he demanded the release of the bull. He knew the Tree women had to be close by now, but how they would act, he could not tell.

He altered his plan and went down into a crouch, heading for the horses and keeping them between himself and the camp. The animals were not disturbed by his nearness. Even when he drew the razor, they continued to eye him trustingly. Silently, with constant glances towards the sleeping men, he sliced through each of the nine tethers. Then he swung away, went around the back of the bull, and headed towards the exit of the underground water course.

Once, long ago, or perhaps even now after a thunderstorm of torrential rain, the mild flowing stream was a raging river that gushed from under the cliff. Thus, the exit of the tunnel was a lot higher than the present water level. The half-breed could step inside by going down into a squat. But the stream was as wide as the tunnel and the water washed around his rump and legs as he backed into the shadows. His hat was crushed against the roof. He halted four feet from the opening and rested the Winchester across his thighs. Then he drew the Colt, held it out at full arm's length, and emptied it towards the horses.

Three shots low, to spurt divots of earth; and three high, to crack close to the heads of the animals. Each bullet discharged from the muzzle in quick succession behind the last as the thumb cocked the hammer and the finger squeezed the trigger. Only the first shot was an isolated sound. All the others were accompanied by the cries of frightened horses and the stamp of their hooves as they were panicked and bolted. Then the yells of alarm of the rudely awakened men. The bull merely swished his tail and stood with a superior look on its face.

By the time the horses had charged away from their cut tethers, Edge had a clear view of the men leaping to their feet, had jerked the Colt out of sight and was spinning the cylinder to drop the expended shellcases into the water. Every man who fisted sleep from his eyes had either a rifle or a revolver in his hand. But the angry and apprehensive eyes saw no target at which to aim although they looked everywhere. The only change in their surroundings from when they bedded down was that it was now daylight and their formerly quiet horses were bolting away from them in all directions.

'Those damn women!' Hollis Millard yelled, twisting this way and that for a sight of Aunt Matty and Muriel.

'Kill 'em this time!' Vic Evans roared, and lunged into a lumbering run towards the bull. He went down on to one knee on the far side of the animal from where Edge was crouched uncomfortably in the river tunnel.

Like his men, he raked his eyes and his gun along the skyline above the low cliff and the humped hill, and towards the forest of rocks into which the stream plunged at the far side of the camp-site. One of the bolting horses had gone splashing along the water course while the others raced across the open ground towards the canyon entrance. But, when there were no more shots and the men ceased to shout, the bolting animals slowed their pace.

Edge slotted fresh shells into the chambers of his Colt and holstered the hand-gun. He steadied the Winchester where it rested across his thighs. Under the belly of the stationary bull he had a perfect shot at the tensely held form of Evans. But he could also see the eight other men, easing upright, as the sun sent its first shaft of yellow light across the jagged tops of the cluster of rocks. The thud of hoof-beats petered out as the runaway horses calmed, and lowered their heads to graze on scattered patches of tough grass.

'What the hell's happenin', Mr Evans?' Clint yelled, a tremor of nervousness in his voice. 'I don't see nobody.'

The big man with the bushy moustache straightened and did a complete turnabout to make a final survey of the high ground on three sides. His face was grim at first, but then he showed a grin.

'So killin' ain't in your bellies, ladies?' he bellowed. 'Well, you ain't got no chance of trickin' me away from this bull.'

He did another turn as he shouted, then stared at his men. 'We're movin' out. Roy, Dale, attend to the bull. You others, pick up your gear and theirs.'

The two men he had named approached him and he stooped to release the padlocks on the shackles. The animal submitted placidly to having the two lariats noosed around his neck. Evans crossed to join the other men who were hefting their bedrolls and saddles. But every man ensured he had a hand free to hold a gun. And eyes constantly raked the surroundings as the group moved towards the scattered horses.

Edge watched the departure with no sense of failure. He had tried and he had lost. But there would be another time.

'Hey, you're goin' the wrong way, Walt!' Clint said. 'I saw your nag head into the rocks.'

Edge had inched forward to keep the men in his range of vision. He saw one man stop and look back apprehensively towards the high, slender pillers of rough-sided rocks. He was a tall, thin man with sunken cheeks and deep-set eyes.

'The women could be in there!' he rasped, and the half-breed recognised the voice. It was the man Clint had roused in the pre-dawn darkness. He shot a pleading look at Evans.

'We're moving out, I said,' Evans told him harshly. 'That was a trick to get us away from the bull, that's all. Go get your horses, Walt. They ain't got the guts for no killin'.'

'Ed?' Walt said, addressing himself to another man with the same build and similar features. 'You wanna give me a hand?'

Ed looked at Evans. 'All right I give my brother some cover, sir?'

The mouth beneath the moustache formed the line of a scornful sneer. 'Sure, if he's that scared of a couple of females. But as soon as we're saddled up we're ridin'. You'll have to catch us up.'

Walt and Ed dropped their gear and carried only their rifles as they made their way back to the camp-site. The others moved to their horses, which were now quiet, and began to saddle them. Edge remained in the damp hiding place, his expression impassive as he watched the two brothers halt at the point where the stream ran noisily into the rocky area. Walt and Ed entered into a low-voiced argument and the man whose horse was missing lost his point. He moved reluctantly into the rocks while his brother remained in the open, pumping the action of his repeater and stiffening as he listened hard.

'Shuddup the lot of you!' Evans snarled, silencing a murmur of disgruntled conversation that had erupted among the men saddling the horses. 'We still got the bull, and that's all that damn well matters.'

Evans was scared. It sounded in his voice for his anger was not strong enough to shield it. Before going through his initial reaction to the menace, he had been too busy to think about what might lie behind the dawn disturbance. Now, with time for his imagination to work, his mind had filled with dread.

'You okay in there, Walt?' Ed shouted.

'Okay, Ed!' Walt responded, his tone a lot lighter than before. 'I see him.'

'What'd I say?' Evans demanded happily. 'Just a trick. Them Tree women ain't got the guts for no killin'.'

Edge shifted slightly to see the main body of men. They were mounted now. Evans, grinning contemptuously at the others, gave his horse a slap on the rump and slammed in his heels to order a gallop. The others chased after him, Roy and Dale trailing with the ropes from the bull lashed around their saddle-horns.

Walt Quincy's horse stood quietly at the side of the rushing water where the stream channelled between two pinnacles of rock. He was chomping on a patch of green, sweet-looking grass. The tall, thin man approached the animal slowly, muttering soft words. The horse continued to graze, and submitted meekly when his owner folded a hand around the bridle.

'Why couldn't you have bolted the same way as the others, you single-minded critter!' the man growled. He turned his head. 'I got him, Ed!'

'So you die happy, skunk!' Mathilda Tree rasped.

'Which Barnaby never did!' Muriel spat.

Walt Quincy whirled, bringing up his Winchester to the level. But he had no chance. He saw Aunt Matty first. She carried a spade, but no gun. Her sister-in-law was aiming the shotgun. Both women stood in the white water shallows where the stream torrented through the rocks, feet firmly planted and eyes staring hatred at the man. He had not even taken first pressure against the Winchester trigger when the shotgun blasted.

The charge took him in the centre of the stomach. It lifted him off his feet and flung him backwards for six feet. Blood and pulpy pieces of flesh and entrails left a broad splash to mark his course. Then he fell hard to the bank of the stream and toppled into the water. The white foam turned pink as it rushed around the legs of the women. The horse reared, whinnied and plunged back the way it had come. Its hoofbeats masked the sound of Ed's voice.

'Walt!' he screamed against the echo of the shotgun blast.

Halfway to the canyon entrance, the riders reined in their mounts and swung in their saddles to stare back towards the site of their night camp. They saw the figure of Ed Quincy unfreeze and lunge forward into the rocks. Perhaps if that was all they had seen, they might have wheeled their horses and galloped them back. But they also saw the familiar tall frame of the half-breed spring out of the river tunnel and launch into a fast run along the bank of the watercourse.

Evans, his face a mask of anger, half drew his rifle from the saddle-boot.

'Don't mess with him!' George Frimley implored. 'Or he'll kill us all!'

Evans's mind raced. The man must have been crouched in the tunnel the whole time after cutting the horses loose. Not more than a few feet away from where he, Evans, had been crouched beside the bull.

'And maybe there ain't just him, Mr Evans!' Clint warned. 'Maybe them women have hired a whole bunch of gunslingers.'

But Evans didn't believe this was likely. If the Tree women had more men than the one man backing them, the escape from the night camp wouldn't have been so easy. 'Let's get!' he snarled, shoving the rifle back in the boot. 'They could pick us off like fish in a barrel from them rocks.'

Again he took the lead at a full gallop in the continued retreat towards the canyon. Edge glanced after the men a moment before he reached the cover of the rocks, going into them several yards to the left of where Ed Quincy had disappeared, where the rush of the torrential water covered his and the noise of Ed's footfalls. But the half-breed had the advantange – Evans's man didn't know he was on the scene.

The forest of rock was like a grey maze, with no passageway more than six feet wide. The morning sun cast shadows, but none deep enough to hide a man. Edge stalked with the Winchester levelled from the hip, his eyes narrowed for a sign of movement and his ears straining to pick up the slightest sound that was not made by the stream. He saw only rock and heard just water. For a full minute. Then:

'You bitches!' Ed Quincy screamed.

He emerged, and stumbled into the stream where his brother had died to see the two women crouched beside the body with the ghastly hole at its centre. The older one was sucking in deep breaths after the effort of hauling the dead weight from the water. The younger was in the process of feeding a fresh shell into the breech of the shotgun. Both spun, still crouched, and froze in terror at the sight of the grief-stricken man aiming a Winchester at them. For a few moments, he too was like a statue, staring at the sodden, blood-stained remains of his brother.

'He killed Barnaby!' Muriel said coldly.

The words snapped the rigidity from Ed Quincy's form and he whipped the rifle stock up against his shoulder to draw a bead on the younger woman.

'Hold it!' Edge rasped.

He had emerged on to the stream bank midway between the man and the two women. Quincy turned instinctively and saw the tall half-breed with the levelled Winchester.

'Drop it, feller,' Edge urged softly.

Quincy looked as if he was ready to comply. But the decision was snatched from him. Walt's Tranter revolver was jutting from the holster on his blood-stained hip. Aunt Matty was nearest to the gun and she drew it before Muriel, Quincy or Edge knew what was happening. The gun had a double action. It exploded in her two-handed grip and the bullet thudded into Quincy's chest. The man, a cheated look on his thin face, dropped his rifle and clutched at the source of his pain. The Tranter fired again. The bullet drove through both Quincy's hands to blast another chest wound. He staggered backwards and started to fall. Aunt Matty fired four more times at the toppling man but these bullets plunged into a dead body. Each wound blossomed crimson and formed a great stain on the shirt-front of the inert man.

Aunt Matty opened her hands to allow the revolver to fall. Then, with a grin of evil pleasure, she looked from Muriel to Edge.

'Makes us even,' she said harshly. 'One each.'

Muriel responded with a nod of satisfaction. Edge showed the old woman a look of murderous contempt. For a few moments, his Winchester was aimed at her. Then he eased the hammer to the rest, canted the rifle across his shoulder and advanced to where the two women were squatting. Both rose to their full heights. Aunt Matty recognised the look on the half-breed's lean face and expressed the same degree of terror as when Ed Quincy had made his presence known. Muriel also recognised the kind of depthless anger that was about to explode from Edge. She snapped the shotgun closed and levelled it from her hip.

'I'll blast you, mister!' she screamed.

Edge halted in mid-stride, six feet from where Aunt Matty had begun to tremble. He lowered his leading foot gently to the ground. His expression slipped into the neutral lines of impassiveness. His tone was utterly flat.

'I warned you about pointing a gun at me, ma'am,' he said, addressing Muriel but fixing his hooded-eyed gaze on Aunt Matty's sweat-beaded face. 'Most folks die if they don't pull the trigger second time they do it.'

'No chance!' Muriel taunted triumphantly.

Edge allowed his body to relax to match his expression and his voice. 'There's a chance,' he answered. 'But I owe you, so you're off the hook.'

'You don't owe me a damn thing!' Muriel snarled.

Edge continued to trap Aunt Matty's fearful gaze. 'I owe you, ma'am. For stopping me doing something I'd regret.'

'Like what?' Sneeringly.

'Smacking the old biddy in the mouth.'

Aunt Matty found her voice. 'He killed my brother,' she excused hoarsely. 'And stood by enjoying it when Evans did that thing with the bull droppings to me.'

Edge gave a curt nod and turned away from both women. 'Neither of them is my concern,' he answered. 'Even if they were, I wouldn't set a feller up to be gunned down that way.'

'So beat it, you squeamish bas—'

'No more, Muriel!' Aunt Matty cut in, recovering the full strength of her voice as she saw the back of the half-breed stiffen. 'He saved our lives. Don't you go losing them for us!'

She swung, reached out, snatched the shotgun from the hands of the younger woman and broke it at the hinge. She softened her tone, speaking to Edge's back.

'Up to you what you do, young feller.' She shook her head.

'But I guess that's your way, anyhow. Like to apologise for what I did. And offer you our thanks for what you did.'

Edge spat, a man removing a bad taste from his mouth. 'Deal stands,' he muttered. 'But with a string. No more warnings. Next time either of you pulls something like that, I'll kill her.'

This time Muriel had no chance to even start an angry retort. A withering glance from the older woman trapped the words in her throat. Edge moved off through the rocks and started to climb the humped hill. He went down the sheer face on the northern side and mounted his horse. He could see the wagon parked at the other end of the gully, where he had dropped the large bundle of coloured threads.

He had to ride in a wide circle around the hill and the area of rocks to reach the abandoned camp. In the time it took, the women had hauled the bodies out from the rocks, dug two graves, lowered the men into the holes and piled the dirt back in. But there were no tombstones on the mounds. The women were gone.

He had rekindled the fire and had shaved, cooked and eaten breakfast by the time the wagon rolled into sight, having travelled the same route as the gelding. The horses of the dead men raised their heads to watch the wagon for a while then continued to graze. With a kind of icy reverence, the women lifted two more tombstones from the rear of the wagon and set them up on the graves.

The sun – halfway to its noon peak now – clearly showed the stark black lettering on the marble.

The women climbed back up on to the seat of the wagon. Aunt Matty winced with rheumatic pain. Muriel bristled with hostility.

'If you're still with us, we'd like you to ride ahead,' the older woman said contritely. 'Could be they'll try to ambush us.'

'Price has gone up,' Edge rasped, finishing a mug of coffee. 'Half what the bull reaches.'

Muriel made a sound of disgust. 'What happened to all that honesty, mister?' She demanded. 'Jacking up the price not included?'

The half-breed poured himself another mug of coffee. 'You

reneged on the deal first, ladies,' he said. 'I said you did your own killing. Seems to me I helped with that last one. And killing's got to come higher than stealing.'

'It's not stealing!' Aunt Matty defended grimly.

'That ain't proved yet. But it sure was killing.' He sipped the coffee.

The women stared away from him to each other. They reached a tacit agreement and Aunt Matty hurried to be the spokeswoman.

'All right. Half.'

Edge tossed the remainder of the coffee on the fire to dampen the ashes, and stood up. 'Obliged, ladies,' he said.

'But not a cent more!' Aunt Matty warned emphatically. 'And Muriel and me play this our way!'

Edge nodded as he packed his gear. 'Just cue me when you plan more killings.'

'So you can run and hide?' Muriel snapped with a contemptuous glare at him.

'Maybe,' the half-breed muttered. 'Seems I've joined Evans and his boys behind the hate ball.'

# Chapter Six

THERE was no ambush in the canyon, or in the foothills beyond to the south-east where the terrain dropped down towards the Colorado River border of Arizona Territory. Edge rode a mile ahead of the wagon, setting a pace that was fast without tiring the horses overmuch. Vic Evans was scared, he had discovered that. And his men had, at first, had no enthusiasm for their job. But the killings could have changed their attitudes. Three of their number had died – building on their fear, perhaps, but at the same time igniting the fires of revenge. Evans could have gained courage from such a changed mood in his men. Or he could have been overruled in his desire to get the bull to its destination in the shortest possible time.

But the half-breed had seen no overt sign of a planned retaliation by Evans and his men by the time he crested a final rise and looked down, through the failing light of dusk, at the town of Mission Creek. He dismounted and waited, watching lamps being lit all over town, until the wagon rolled to a halt just before it would be silhouetted on the ridge.

'What's down there?' Muriel asked sourly.

Edge pursed his lips. 'Trouble, maybe. Or just information. Like to take a look on my own.'

The older woman was suffering from muscular pains again and remained on the high seat. Muriel climbed down to the ground and moved forward to join Edge. Her green eyes, as devoid of emotion as the half-breed's, surveyed what lay at the foot of the hill. A town of four streets, laid out as if for a gigantic game of tic-tac-toe. One of the streets formed a section of a trail stretching from north to south. Another opened out on to a trail which snaked away to the east, following the course of the creek, which was now dry. The terrain to the north, south and east was flat, featured with a scattering of small farms. It was around supper time and there was no traffic on the streets.

'If they're watching, they'd see the wagon coming in,' she said at the conclusion of her careful survey.

'And I figured all you could think about was killing, ma'am.'

She glared at him. 'Mathilda and I will wait here for you.'

He swung into the saddle. 'You ought to be able to think of something better to do.'

He heeled the horse forward, over the crest of the hill and down towards Mission Creek. There was no marker on the slope or on the west side of the town, but he knew its name from seeing the tattered map the women were using to plan their route to El Paso. From studying that same map, he knew that the creek for which the town was named ran eastwards for three miles before joining the Colorado River. Once across this obstacle, he would be in familiar territory. Arizona, where he had committed a mass murder just a few short weeks after the slaughter of war was finished. A series of five brutal slayings which should have given him an affinity with the women waiting at the top of the hill. For the five men had died because they gunned down his brother; and now ten men had been marked for death because they killed somebody's brother and somebody else's husband. But there was no affinity: for such a condition demanded human feeling and that was something the lone rider who entered Mission Creek was unable to give.

The evening was warm and still. The appetising aromas of cooking food hung in the air, mixed with the more acrid taint of wood-smoke. Lamps dropped welcoming wedges of light from windows. The sound of the gelding's hooves hitting the dusty street in a slow walk competed only with the occasional burst of loud laughter from the saloon on a corner where two streets met at an intersection. It was from the windows and over the batswing doors that the brightest light in town came. Two horses were hitched to the rail outside. Old and broken down stallions carrying ancient and ill-cared-for saddles. But a lot more than two voices contributed to the noise issuing from the saloon.

'You the man they been expectin'?'

Edge reined his horse to a halt and narrowed his eyes to look ahead and to the left. More than one pair of boots scraped on the hollow sidewalk. Four men stepped down into the street to be caught in the glow of light spilling from windows on the other side. One of them was about fifty. The other three were in their late twenties or early thirties. All of them wore gunbelts with holsters strapped to their legs. The metal of the guns glinted with a duller light than the stars pinned to their shirt fronts.

'Law for sale in Mission Creek?' Edge asked evenly.

The trio of younger men stiffened. The older, shorter man sighed. 'You got trouble with them seven guys rode in earlier, son. You don't want none with me and my deputies.'

Edge showed a cold grin. 'Always prefer it when the local law's agreeable,' he said.

'It ain't for sale here, son. It's for keepin' the peace. You start disturbin' it and the town drunk gets let out a day early. Ain't got but the one cell in the gaolhouse. Mission Creek's a law-abidin' town.'

'Room for seven if they start the action, feller?'

The sheriff sighed again. 'Be a tight squeeze, but we won't be worryin' too much about 'em being comfortable.'

Edge nodded and clucked the gelding forward.

'What about the women they said about?' he heard one of the deputies rasp.

'Ain't our concern unless they cross town limits,' the sheriff responded flatly.

The half-breed angled his horse across the intersection and slid from the saddle. The men in the saloon continued to enjoy themselves. He hitched the reins around the rail and stepped heavily on the sidewalk. The laughter and talk was abruptly curtailed, and Edge's head and shoulders above the batswings became the centre of attention.

It was a big saloon, furnished with the bare essentials. A bar with bottle-lined shelves along one side and a scattering of chairs and tables using up a large proportion of the remaining space. There was a dusty piano in one corner, and light was forcing its way through the smoke-laden atmosphere from half a dozen oil lamps hung from ceiling beams. Evans and his six men were lined up at the bar. The plump bartender was in the process of pouring them fresh drinks. All the hilarity had apparently been coming from a group of four old-timers sitting at a table, playing cards for dead matches. Then three of the Evans hands – not the man with the moustache himself – made a move for their guns.

'Be happy to let the drunk serve out his time,' the half-breed called evenly, draping a hand over his holstered gun in the cover of the doors.

From the expression that spread upon the faces of the seven men, he knew they had received the same warning from the dour lawman.

'You alone?' Evans rasped as Edge pushed open the doors and stepped into the saloon.

'You see anybody else, feller?'

'We didn't see *nobody* this mornin'.'

Edge bellied up to the bar ten feet away from the last man in the line of Evans men. This was a nervous George Frimley. He stared at his image reflected between two bottles by a mirror. 'Two guys learned too late it pays to stay alert,' he answered. 'Cold beer when you're ready, bartender.'

'Coming right up, sir,' the man said quickly, and hurried to finish his current order.

The old-timers returned to their card game, but made less noise now.

'George, Clint, go look after the bull!' Evans snapped. 'I don't like this set up.'

'But the sheriff and his dep – ' Frimley began.

'Do like I say!' Evans snarled. 'No tellin' what them two females got up their sleeves.'

The two men sank their shots of whiskey fast and heaved away from the bar, as the bartender drew a foaming beer and placed the glass in front of Edge, who slammed some coins on the countertop.

'Obliged to you.'

'My pleasure, sir.'

The sound of the beer passing down the half-breed's throat was the only sound in the saloon after Clint and Frimley had pushed out through the batswings. The old-timers began to whisper their calls and antes. The bartender worked industriously at polishing glasses. Some of Evans's men shuffled their feet.

'Whatever them women are payin' you I'll double it if you'll leave them to – '

'You can't afford it feller,' Edge cut in evenly on the blurting voice of Evans. 'Getting half that beef on the hoof.'

'Jesus!' Hollis Millard gasped.

'That's crazy,' said Ray Irwin, the man with the broken nose.

Evans recovered his composure after the shock. 'Twenty-five grand?' he sneered. 'Sounds cheap for killin' ten men.'

'Another one, bartender,' Edge called, pushing his empty glass away from him. 'Women do their own killing, feller. That thing back at Railton – that was personal.'

'So what the hell's worth twenty-five thousand?' Evans demanded.

'Half the bull.' The beer was drawn and set down in front of Edge. The bartender counted some coins from the pile of change on the counter top.

'My bull!' Evans roared, and drew his Colt.

He was three men away from Edge and hidden from the half-breed by them. Edge saw just Evans's face crimson with anger as he leaned forward to stare along the burned and gouged counter top. The three men hurriedly backed up. And those behind followed suit. Edge remained bellied up to the counter and turned just his head to look at the man with the moustache. Evans's complexion as he pivoted, shaded into purple.

'You figure to steal my bull?' His voice was thick and spittle dribbled from the corner of his mouth.

He was trembling with rage but his gun-hand, which rested on the counter top, was as steady as a rock. He squeezed the trigger and a bullet exploded from the gun. The lead shattered the glass in front of Edge, spraying shards along the scarred wood and spilling beer in every direction. The half-breed remained where he was, as unmoving as a stone carving. His hooded eyes, which did not blink at the sound of the shot, directed a look of sneering scorn at Evans.

'Another beer, bartender,' he said evenly. 'Better have a fresh glass. This feller will pay.'

Nobody moved for long seconds. Then, as heavy footfalls hit the sidewalk outside, the bartender unfroze.

'Comin' right up, sir.'

The old-timers and Evans's men stared in expectant silence, awaiting the next explosive move.

'Whatever them women told you, it was lies!' Evans snarled. 'I got legal entitlement to that animal.'

The batswings crashed open and the sheriff led his trio of deputies into the saloon at a run. They pulled up short, in a menacing line, with right hands close to gun butts.

'Who fired that gun?' the sheriff demanded.

Evans was still resting his hand on the counter top, palm wrapped round the Colt butt. Edge accepted the replacement beer and raised it to his lips. He eyed his reflection in the mirror and spoke over the rim of the glass.

'Possession's nine points of the law, sheriff,' he said. 'That feller happens to be holding the bull and the gun.'

'I warned you guys!' the lawman snarled. 'All of you!'

'No harm done!' the bartender said quickly. 'A glass got broke, that's all.'

'Peace got broke,' the sheriff countered. 'I ought to throw the whole bunch of you in the gaolhouse, that's what I ought to do.'

His grim-faced deputies nodded their approval.

'But I ain't gonna do that.'

The younger lawmen expressed their disapproval.

'Gonna ask you to leave Mission Creek.' He sighed. 'And if you don't do like I ask – right quick – gonna run you out.'

Edge finished his drink and lowered the glass. 'Only here for the beer,' he said as he turned and strolled towards the door.

The sheriff, wearing a look of suspicion, waited until the last moment before he stepped aside. As the doors swung closed behind the tall, lean figure, Evans thrust the Colt back into his holster and got a stricken look on to his face.

'The bull!' he exclaimed, raking his eyes along the faces of his men, then started forward. His men made to move in behind him. But the whole group pulled up short as the sheriff stepped back into the line of deputies.

'No more trouble!'

Evans spat on to the sawdust-covered floor. 'Not in this jerk-water town, unless they start it.'

The sheriff nodded, and stepped aside gesturing for his fellow lawmen to do likewise. Evans led his men out on to the street with the peace officers hard on their heels.

'Hey,' one of the old-timers called to the bartender. 'You didn't collect for that other beer, Matt.'

Matt looked relieved as he started to pick shards of splinters off his counter top. 'Happy to lose just the price of a beer in the kinda trouble that's brewin' there,' he answered.

'Already been brewed, I'm thinkin',' another of the old-timers said reflectively. 'Bein' stirred now. Deal the cards, Augie.'

Edge had mounted the gelding and was riding him back west along the street at an easy walk as the men burst from the saloon behind him. He glanced over his shoulder at the sound of their footfalls on the sidewalk, but they did not come after him. Instead, as the four lawmen halted at the centre of the intersection, Evans and his hands streamed along the north-bound street.

'Clint!' Evans yelled. 'Everythin' all right?'

The half-breed felt eyes watching him as he rode between the lamp-lit windows of the houses. But he didn't respond to the half fearful, half curious examination. Instead, he concentrated upon the crest of the hill, where the wagon was silhouetted against the dark sky, the team motionless in the traces. A small group of people stood at the side of the wagon – two women and two men. Over such a distance in a low light level, it was impossible to discern more than the dark forms of the quartet. But Edge had only to know the number to know their identities. Muriel Tree had taken his advice about doing more than merely waiting on the hill top.

'Hey, mister!' Clint yelled in terror as Edge started up the hillside.

'Tell 'em to stop this!' George Frimley shrieked. 'It's cold-blooded murder!'

Edge did not reply.

'What the hell's happenin'?' the sheriff of Mission Creek demanded, breaking into a lumbering run in the wake of Edge. His deputies chased after him.

'Evans!' It was Muriel's voice, shrill and piercing. 'Evans, you murdering bastard!'

Edge reined the gelding to a halt on the lower slope. The lawmen skidded to a breathless stop a few yards behind him. Windows were thrown open and heads poked out. Doors creaked and figures stepped into the wedges of light.

'You *are* with the women!' the sheriff accused.

The half-breed continued to look up at the hill crest. 'I break any town ordinances, feller?' he asked.

'You sure as hell kept them guys busy while the women snuck into Mission Creek.'

'And stole the bull, I'm thinkin',' a deputy added.

'Evans show you proof he owns the bull?' Edge wanted to know.

'I didn't ask, stranger. But you called it about possession being nine points of the law.'

'Mr Evans, help us?' Clint pleaded, full-throated.

Edge nodded. 'So if the women have got possession . . . ?'

'They ain't!'

The deputy's response caused Edge to swing in the saddle and look over the lawmen's turned heads, back along the street to the intersection. Evans, Hollis Millard, Jeb, Ray and Dale had moved back into sight. Ray and Dale had assumed their familiar roles of being in charge of the stud bull.

'Sheriff, there's gonna be murder done if you don't stop it!' Evans yelled.

A cold anger glinted in Edge's eyes as he returned his attention to the top of the hill.

'He right?' the lawman asked to the half-breed's rigidly set back.

'So you can see what's comin' to you, Vic Evans!' Aunt Matty bellowed.

'Move, you bastards!' From Muriel.

'Run, skunks!' From her sister-in-law.

The skinny Clint and the overweight George Frimley were helped on their way with a prod in the back from their own rifles. They stumbled forward, found their strides and broke into a balanced run. They screamed their terror. The fat man ran in a straight line. Clint began to zigzag. Frimley was hit first, a dozen yards from his murderer. A bullet from the rifle in Aunt Matty's hands smashed into the back of his skull and ripped through his left eye, trailing gore that gleamed in the moonlight. Clint took a bullet in the right hip and spun to the ground. He fell lengthwise across the slope and started to roll. Muriel pumped the repeater's action and squeezed the trigger. The second shot missed and she tried again. And again; and a fourth time. There were no more misses. Clint was hit in the back once and the stomach twice. Three trails of blood linked where he had tumbled to where he came to rest.

'Looks like,' Edge muttered in reply to the lawman's question.

There were gasps and grunts of horror from the watching citizens of Mission Creek.

'Arrest 'em, sheriff!' Evans shrieked. 'Them women and Edge! You saw it! Two unarmed men gunned down in the back!'

The half-breed had his cold rage under control as he turned again in his saddle to survey the lawmen. Three of them expressed dumbstruck contempt. The other looked as if he was going to be sick.

'For stealing a bull?' a deputy managed to rasp.

'That was after they killed a husband and brother.'

'Where?' the sheriff asked.

'Up north. Far as you can go before you're in a foreign country.'

'Sheriff!' Hollis Millard yelled. 'You gonna do like Mr Evans said?'

He, Evans and Jeb started along the street from the intersection. Ray and Dale held back, the bull trapped between them on two lines.

'Women won't be no trouble,' a deputy pointed out, nodding up the hill.

His words and gesture called all attention back to Aunt Matty and Muriel. The two women had set down the rifles and were starting over the crest, each carrying a shovel and a tombstone.

'They gonna bury them guys?' the sheriff demanded, incredulously.

Edge took out the makings and watched the approach of Evans and his two men as he rolled a cigarette. 'Provide everything except a preacher,' he answered.

'Well?' Evans demanded. Millard and Jeb flanked him. All three held their right hands low, poised for the draw. 'You do anythin' 'cept talk about keepin' peace in this town?'

Edge lit the cigarette and hung it at the corner of his mouth. He hooked the thumb of his right hand over his gunbelt, an inch or so in front of the jutting Colt butt. And he eased his feet from the stirrups.

'This town ends just about where you guys are standing,' the lawman answered frowning after a few moments thought. 'And I'm town law. Not county.'

The women had reached the slumped body of George Frimley. They set down the tombstone and began to thud their shovels into the hillside.

'You mean you're goin' to let these three killers get away with what you just saw?' Evans snarled.

Edge and the lawmen were some ten yards away from the trio of incensed men. The sheriff moved first, but his deputies were quick to follow. They halted behind Evans and his two hands.

'Asked you to leave Mission Creek,' the sheriff reminded. 'One more step the way you're facin' and what happens then ain't none of my business. Or you can head the other way and pick up your horses as you pass through.'

Evans swung his angry eyes away from the detached expression on the sheriff's face, glared at the women engaged in their grave-digging, then fixed them on Edge.

'You said killin' ain't part of your deal, right?' he rasped.

Edge nodded. 'Right feller.'

Evans took the single step over the imaginary town line and drew his gun. But Edge drew at the same time and fired while the man on the ground was still cocking his weapon. The bullet gouged across the top of Evans's thumb and cut a furrow along his hand from the knuckle to the wrist. The Colt fell through the spray of blood. Millard and the other men had started to reach for their guns, but they snatched their hands away.

Aunt Matty and Muriel glanced up from their chore, then resumed it. There were some more gasps from the watchers. Evans sucked at his bleeding wound and glared up at the mounted, half-turned half-breed with pain and rage.

'Just friggin' woundin'!' he croaked, spitting out blood.

'No part of the deal, feller. You spilled my beer.'

Evans began to shake with frustration. He shifted his stare from Edge to the gravedigging women. Then he swung his head from one side to the other, glowering at his men. 'Hollis, Jeb. he ain't got nothing against you. Blast them females before they get us all.'

The fat Jeb eyed the women and licked his lips. But then he glanced at Hollis Millard for a lead and found the man was nervously appraising Edge.

'Not me,' Millard said. 'No, sir, Mr Evans. He might figure I looked at him the wrong way some time.'

He swung around and moved hurriedly along the street. Jeb paused only a moment before following him. Evans was shaking so badly now he seemed on the point of collapse. But he brought himself under control. Enough to stoop, snatch up his Colt in his left hand and storm away in the wake of his men.

Edge pushed his Colt back into the holster and took the cigarette from his mouth, spitting a piece of loose tobacco off his lip.

The sheriff let out his breath in a noisy sigh. 'You got anything against those other two guys?' he asked curiously.

'Not a thing.'

'So they could've blasted the women?' the sick-looking deputy croaked.

'Same as Evans, if he can shoot left-handed,' Edge answered, dropping the half-smoked cigarette.

'You're a real generous guy,' another deputy said sourly. 'Only shoot a man once for spillin' your beer.'

'Real fancy shootin' though,' a watching citizen called. 'Pow!' He struck the heel of one hand across the back of another in imitation of a bullet furrowing Evans's flesh.

'Comes of being brought up in a poor family,' Edge muttered, and clucked his horse forward as he turned in the saddle. 'Always looking for a hand out.'

## Chapter Seven

'ONLY five of the skunks left now,' Aunt Matty said with a sigh of satisfaction, between digging shovelfuls of earth out of the grave.

Edge had halted the gelding a few feet short of where the women were working. He had been watching silently for long moments, as the audience at the foot of the hillside dispersed. He still said nothing.

'And we got to thank you again, young feller. Evans would have come gunning for us if you hadn't blasted the pistol out of his hand.'

'I bet you he didn't do that for us, Aunt Matty,' Muriel said, panting; not interrupting her work with the shovel.

'Right,' Edge said sourly. 'How'd you get those two out of town?'

The older woman grinned. 'By pointing the shotgun at them, that's how. Came like lambs.'

'Couldn't scare the bull though, uh?'

Hoofbeats sounded from below and they all looked down upon Mission Creek. All the citizens and the four lawmen were off the streets now. Evans and his diminished bunch of men were heading out of town towards the trail stretching out into the east.

Muriel rested her shovel for a moment and spat on her

hands. 'You're in for half, mister,' she reminded grimly. 'But you got to do more to earn it than drink beer while Aunt Matty and me go hunting. You made the deal. We do the killing. Seems to us you ought to get the bull.'

She went to work again.

'Besides which,' Aunt Matty added. 'We couldn't handle the men and that ornery critter all at once.'

'Specially not when you're frightened to go near him.' Muriel accused.

'He's out to get me, I tell you,' the older woman countered. 'He hates me, I know it.'

Edge dismounted and led the gelding up to the wagon. Behind him, the women ended their mild quarrel almost as soon as it began and devoted all their energies to the gravedigging. The half-breed fed and watered the team and his own horse, then set a fire and made coffee. He ate from his supplies and climbed into the rear of the wagon to bed down on the scattered hay.

He was jolted awake when the wagon jerked into motion, canting over the crest of the hill and starting down, with the wheels skidding as the brake stayed locked on. He peered over the tail-gate and saw that his unsaddled gelding was hitched to the wagon. The fire had been doused. Lower down, he saw the two mounds with the familiar tombstones positioned on top. The wagon slithered on to a diagonal course, angling towards the north-east. He peered around the side and saw they were heading on a route to by-pass Mission Creek.

'We figured they wouldn't give us no welcome if we rolled through, young feller.'

Aunt Matty's ugly face was visible as she leaned away from the seat to look back along the side of the wagon. Even in the pale light of the moon it was possible to see how much the digging chore had taken out of her pain-wracked body. Her face was haggard, the eyes sunken and, as she grinned, her features took on the aspect of a death mask.

'Only feller who would thank you is the town drunk,' Edge said, and withdrew into the wagon. He checked that the booted Winchester on the saddle was within reach, and lay back, tipping his hat over his face. He had slept in more discomfort than aboard a rolling wagon, and it took just a couple of minutes to sink into shallow unconsciousness again.

The wagon reached the Colorado river, reduced by drought to a mild trickle of muddy water. On the far bank, the trail swung south-west across a desert plain towards the point where the Gila Bend and the Big Horn Mountain ranges formed a broad valley. Edge continued to sleep. Muriel Tree drove the team while her sister-in-law watched the ground ahead for signs left by their quarry. Midnight was a half-hour gone when the lead horse on the left went lame.

Edge came awake for the second time that night as Aunt Matty moved to the rear of the wagon and peered at him over the tail-gate.

'We're surrounded by Apaches and you want to know what to do,' he muttered from under his hat.

'Injuns we could handle.'

'Same as the Evans hands, uh?'

'Right, young feller. But we got us a lame horse.'

Edge eased up into a sitting position and straightened his hat on his head. 'How lame?'

'He won't be doing no more walkin'.'

The half-breed eased himself over the tail-gate and down to the ground. 'So shoot him,' he said, surveying the surrounding country. It consisted of rolling, sparsely vegetated low hills.

Aunt Matty's face, more haggard than ever, expressed concern. She shook her head. 'Dumb animals ain't like Evans and his men.'

Edge spat the foul taste of sleeping from his mouth. 'Way they been letting you pick them off, ma'am, they're a lot like dumb animals, I'd say.'

'Will you do it?'

Edge led the way to the front of the wagon, where Muriel was taking the lame horse out of the team. The stallion was limping badly, and snorted when he put his left forehoof to the ground. His flesh was lathered with the sweat of pain. As the man approached and the woman released him, the animal went down, front end first, and rolled on to his side. His nostrils flared as he panted. As Edge squatted and stroked the horse's neck, the two women turned away. The half-breed drew his gun and talked softly to the distressed animal as he rested the muzzle between the bulging eyes. He squeezed the trigger and the shot rolled away across the hills to be swallowed up by the night. The carcase twitched once and became still.

'Thank you, Mr Edge,' Muriel said, the sentiment genuine and her tone surprisingly soft.

The half-breed delivered the stock answer. 'Didn't do it for you. It was the animal that was suffering.' He eyed the three other stallions, which had failed to react to the sudden shot in the stillness. 'And you'd better move off aways from him and make camp or you'll likely lose some more.'

Not for the first time, the women followed the man's advise. They led the team at a walk over the brow of the next low rise and halted at the foot of it to bed down for the night. Edge paused on the higher ground, to peer across the moon-bathed landscape. He saw nothing, but he did not ignore the hunch that had come to him a moment after he shot the lame horse. No matter how afraid Evans and his men were, there had to come a time when they would begin to fight back. Even the most innocuous animal will turn upon its predator and become a fierce fighter when cornered. To survive.

Out here in the wilderness, wide and open, the remaining five men with the bull could in no way be termed cornered. But they were struggling to survive the murderous wrath of the women who had stuck doggedly to their footsteps for so long. Half their number were now buried beneath the ominous tombstones. Slowed to a pace dictated by the bull – the reason for the long treck – they had to realise, eventually, that they could not outrun their pursuers.

And, an unexplained shot in the night behind them might be the trigger they needed to swing them from defence to attack.

These were the thoughts which were running through the half-breed's mind as he raked his slit-eyed gaze over the unmoving country to the south-west. Evans and his four men would be camped out there somewhere. In the utter stillness of the night, the sound of the shot would have carried at least ten miles. Maybe farther, to ears that were attuned to pick up the slightest noise which would indicate danger.

'Something on your mind, young feller?' Aunt Matty said as she was about to crawl into the tent. Muriel was already inside.

'You've had it too easy, is all,' he replied as he went to the rear of the wagon and drew the Winchester from the saddle-boot resting inside. 'One dead horse against five dead men. Lady Luck ain't going to keep blowing on your dice like that much longer.'

Aunt Matty sank to the ground outside the tent, grimacing as a leg bent awkwardly. She sighed. 'You probably noticed how Evans and me seem kind of chummy on occasions, young feller. Me calling him Vic and him calling me Mathilda?'

'Ain't been listening much to what either of you say,' Edge answered evenly.

'Him and me lived in the same town all our lives. His spread's a lot bigger than the Tree farm, but we was neighbours. Got to know each other real well.' She grimaced, but not from pain this time. 'And there ain't no worse coward walking God's earth, I'm tellin' you. His pa had to fight all his battles for him, at first. Then, when the old man Evans passed on, why Vic would go ten miles out of his way to avoid trouble of any kind. But, if there was no way round trouble, then he'd make sure he was backed up by those nine hands of his.'

'Playing poker with a cold deck is a lot closer than ten miles to trouble, ma'am,' the half-breed pointed out.

A sour grin replaced the grimace on the ugly, draw face. 'Barnaby was a couple of inches higher than five feet and most of the time he was drunk. And the only gun he ever carried was the one they strapped on him after they pumped ten slugs into him. Barnaby was only trouble to himself.'

'He was a good man,' Muriel said sadly from inside the tent. 'No husband could have treated a wife better than he did me.'

The older woman sighed and showed Edge a wan smile. 'That ends the conversation, I'm thinkin',' she said, and turned to crawl into the tent. 'This young feller don't like talkin' about marriage.'

'What'll you do if they come, mister?' Muriel called.

'My end of the deal is to get the bull,' Edge answered as he turned from the tent.

'And me and Aunt Matty can get killed asleep while you're taking care of your end?'

'I'll see you get buried decent,' he called back softly as he started up the hill from which he had made his unproductive survey. 'But I travel light. Didn't bring no marble markers with me.'

At the top of the hill he raked his eyes across the terrain once more, with the same result. He sat down on his haunches to wait, back a little from the crest to avoid being silhouetted on the skyline. The women had eaten a cold supper, without coffee. So there was no fire to provide a beacon for potential attackers. Evans and his men would not need a guiding light, though. All they had to do was backtrack on their own trail.

Only three of them came – two hours after Edge had taken his position on top of the rise. He saw them when they were still a long way off – a trio of moving shadows on the otherwise unmoving landscape. He saw them crest two humps of high ground and go from sight while still mounted. When they appeared again they were leading their horses. The next time he spotted them they were minus their mounts. They were moving in a half-crouched attitude, rifles at the ready: stalking.

Edge glanced down at the quiet camp, then eased backwards, down the side of the hill where the decomposing carcase of the shot horse lay. When he was out of danger of being silhouetted, he rose erect and began to run. To his left for a hundred yards, then he turned left again, still running. Thus, he went around the hill. Another rise forced him even farther away from where the women slept and where the Evans men were closing in on them. He slowed his pace and dropped down on to all fours as he started up a slope which had no convenient way around it. At the top, he went out flat on to his belly: only his head raised so that his hooded eyes could survey the terrain. After a few moments he caught sight of the hat of the tallest man in the trio. It was in view for only a couple of seconds, between two humps on a hill crest. But this was enough to show Edge that at least one of Evans's men had just a single hill to go over before he would see the camp. He was already closer to the women than Edge.

The half-breed waited perhaps five seconds, peering intently in every direction. But nothing moved until he did, going forward on a new course: down one slope and up another towards the point where he had seen the hat. When he reached the twin humps, a cold grin parted his thin lips and sharpened the glint in his narrowed eyes. The three men were sticking together as they advanced up the final hill towards their objective. He was behind them now, about fifty yards away from them across a small valley formed by the two hills. Close enough to see the tense way in which the men put one foot in front of the other, the rigid attitudes of their slightly arched backs and the forward-thrusting positions of their heads and rifles. He had seen enough of the Evans hands to recognise these three. Hollis Millard, Ray Irwin and Dale. That meant the pudgy Jeb and the tall Evans were taking care of the bull. Or moving in on the camp from another direction?

Edge discounted this possibility as he slowly stood up and started silently in the wake of the trio. Evans would not leave the bull unguarded. And the last of his hands? If somebody was moving in alone on a different line of approach, it would not be the nervous Jeb.

He reached the foot of the hill before the Evans men reached the top. Then he dropped into a crouch, bringing the stock of the Winchester up to his shoulder to draw a bead on the back of the tallest man – Hollis Millard. A few moments later, the men reached the vantage point from where they could see the camp, and then powered down into crouches. Low gasps accompanied the movements.

'We found 'em!' Irwin rasped.

Because the three were crouched on the same side of the hill as he, Edge could hear their soft-voiced conversation, but the brow of the rise would prevent the sound carrying down into the hollow beyond.

'Yeah!' Dale responded.

Millard rose slightly and peered in every direction. The pale moonlight showed his face was as strained as his physical attitude had been. His eyes raked the surrounding hill crests, sweeping high over the spot where Edge was crouched, one shadow among many.

'What you . . . ' Irwin started.

'Edge,' Millard cut in, sinking down to the ground again. 'I don't see that bastard beddin' down without fixin' a watch.'

'For what?' Dale muttered scornfully. 'We ain't given *him* no trouble before.'

Millard bellied forward to peer down at the camp again.

'Maybe that was what the shot was?' Irwin suggested. 'Could be the Tree women blasted him.'

Millard looked back over his shoulder. 'Figure it was a horse got shot. Only four down there now.'

'Edge took off?' Dale suggested.

'His nag's there,' Millard countered. 'One of the team that's missin'.'

Irwin spat and it was the loudest sound so far. 'We gonna sit here yakkin' all damn night?' he growled.

'I ain't,' Dale came back, low but emphatic.

He and Irwin looked at each other and rose to their full heights, stepping up to the top of the hill. Millard eased up between them. It was he who issued the order.

'You two blast the tent. I'll take the wagon. If he's there, that's where he'll be bedded down.'

As they raised the rifles to their shoulders, Edge stood upright. 'Really are looking at me the wrong way now, feller,' he snapped out.

All three men were standing close together and they whirled in the same direction at the same time. This meant that Dale's rifle barrel cracked against Millard's shoulder as Millard's gun hit Irwin. Thus, Irwin was the only man to draw a bead on the half-breed.

'Get him!' Millard screamed.

Irwin was squeezing the trigger before the words were spoken. But Edge was an instant faster, having altered his aim from the man at the centre to the one on the right. His bullet slammed into Irwin's stomach travelling upwards, bringing a grunt from the man. It penetrated a lung before slamming to a halt against a broken rib. Irwin's rifle pumped a bullet into the ground at his feet as he fell forward, spewing a crimson gush from his gaping mouth.

'Dear God!' Dale moaned, watching in rigid horror as the body of Irwin tumbled limply down the slope.

Millard's reaction to the bloody death was more positive. As the body fell, allowing his rifle to complete its arc, he powered down into a crouch. His repeater was already cocked. Edge had to pump the action of the Winchester. Both guns exploded simultaneously. Millard's bullet punched a hole in the brim of the half-breed's hat and Edge felt a smarting pain on his shoulder blade as the lead tore his shirt and skimmed across the skin beneath. His own bullet followed the precise line of Millard's rifle barrel, pinged against the top of the frame and spun into the man's sighting eye. He was dead an instant after the impact, flung backwards out of the crouch to fall out of sight over the brow of the hill as his freed rifle slithered down towards Edge.

The half-breed pivoted a few degrees as he pumped the Winchester's action again. Dale had unfroze from his immoblising terror. But his rifle was still held low as Edge covered him. He dropped the weapon as though it was something vile and thrust his hands high into the air.

'Don't shoot!' he screamed.

'That you, Edge!' Aunt Matty called. The intervening high ground made her voice sound a long way off. 'We got him covered this side.'

'Please?' Dale begged.

'Forget the guns and break out the markers,' Edge called as he lowered the Winchester and started up the hill. 'Just two.'

'Like hell two!' Muriel Tree bellowed. 'Dale Bately's as guilty as the rest of them!'

New fear took control of Bately and he began to tremble. The shaking showed most plainly in his upraised arms. His head turned and his wide eyes stared out of a contorted face down towards the women.

'I'll kill you for sure!' Edge snarled.

He quickened his pace to reach the top of the hill, swerving to avoid the slumped form of Ray Irwin. He emerged on to the crest six feet to one side of the terrified Bately. Aunt Matty was no threat to anybody. She held a revolver – aimed at Bately but with no chance of hitting him over such a range. Muriel had the stock of the shotgun hard against her shoulder. Her cheek was pressed to the polished wood and her finger was curled around the trigger. If she fired the gun, its charge would scatter. Shot would hit both men. Maybe neither would die, but both would be in a bad mess.

'Bately!' the younger woman yelled. 'Tell this guy how my husband was cheated and murdered!'

The Evans hand trusted himself to move slightly. With his hands still stretching shakily towards the night sky, he shifted his feet so that he was facing Edge. His mouth opened and closed several times before any words emerged.

'He was one of them in the poker game along with Evans and Walt Quincy!' Aunt Matty accused. 'He knows for sure.'

Her voice covered the hoarse whisper vented from Bately's spittle-run lips.

'Tell him!' Muriel screamed.

'He's trying,' Edge said evenly. 'But he can't get a word in Edge ways.'

'We didn't know about the marked deck,' Bately managed to force out. 'Mr Evans didn't say anthin' until after the game was finished.'

'And you didn't know your gun was loaded when you aimed it at Barnaby and pulled the trigger?' Muriel snarled.

It was plain she and the older woman were willing to believe the story of the card game. But the more dangerous truth was already well known. Bately's eyes pleaded for the half-breed's help. And he lowered his arms and stretched them out towards Edge. 'Tree was on Evans land,' he moaned. 'And we all work for Evans. We gave him fair warnin', mister. But he just kept on comin'. When Mr Evans told us to fire, we had to.'

'And the gun, you skunk?' Aunt Matty demanded. 'My stupid kid brother never did wear a gun!'

Bately gulped. 'Mr Evans said it would look better if Tree had a gun when we took him into town. He strapped one on him.'

'All right, Mr High-and-Mighty Edge?' Muriel snarled. 'Gunning down an unarmed man? Don't that mean he should pay?'

Edge ignored the question. 'Where's Evans, the other feller and the bull?' he asked Bately.

The man looked back the way he and his two partners had come. 'Headin' for El Paso. Me and Hollis and Ray, we were gettin' real mad the way our men have been gettin' killed. We figured to make a stand, but Mr Evans and Jeb Stuart, they weren't for that. They were pushin' on. Tryin' to outrun you people.'

'So you and the others decided to sneak up on us and kill us while we were sleepin'?' Aunt Matty accused.

Bately seemed about to whirl towards the women and yell a retort. But he quashed the impulse and continued to plead with his eyes directed at Edge. 'That any worse than what they did to Clint and George back at Mission Creek?' he asked. 'And I bet the Quincys didn't have any more of a chance in the rocks.'

The half-breed backed away from Bately, twisting his wrist to cant the Winchester across his shoulder. He raised his right hand to join the left fisted around the frame of the rifle.

'Quincys had a gun, like you, feller,' he replied, having widened the gap to ten feet. Not loud, but loud enough to reach the ears of the women.

'You mean – ?' Bately started to ask as Edge continued to back away from him.

'Do what you damn well like, Edge!' Muriel challenged.

She squeezed the shotgun's trigger. As the report split the night and the muzzle flash momentarily dimmed the moonlight, the half-breed threw himself to the ground – to his left to put some solid earth between himself and the deadly blast. Bately whirled and dragged in his hands to claw the revolver from his holster. He got off a shot that went wide. Aunt Matty's first shot went high. So did the centre of the scattering charge that was belched from the muzzle of the shotgun. But Bately's head was caught by the lower curve of pellets. He screamed, high and thin, as tiny grains of metal pelted into his face. His eyes were pulped into blindness by the assault. His forehead was cleaned of flesh down to the bone. His cheeks, jaw and throat were abruptly sheened with bright crimson as blood pumped from countless tiny, deep wounds.

But the will for revenge kept him on his feet – and even started him into a crazed run down the hillside. Unable to see, he charged towards the women instinctively, his scream becoming a deeper, more powerful sound of hatred. Edge, his head raised to watch, looked at the scene with cold silence. Muriel Tree had broken open the shotgun and was fumbling a new cartridge into the breech. Six feet away from her, Mathilda Tree held the revolver out in front of her, at the full stretch of both arms as she clutched the gun in her usual double-handed grip. As he ran, the horribly-wounded man started to fan his Colt, raking it from side to side.

The older woman fired again – and for a second time failed to find her target. The bullet cracked close over the half-breed's head.

'See why you prefer to be called Miss Tree,' he growled.

It was the final shot exploding from Bately's gun that half finished the job he and his two partners had come to do. It hit Muriel Tree in the right hip and she collapsed to her knees, dropping the freshly-loaded shotgun to the ground in front of her.

'Mathilda!' she shrieked above the snorting of the rearing horses.

Aunt Matty started to use the double action of her revolver. Bately was knocked out of his crazed charge by a bullet in the stomach. He folded forward, lost his footing and went into a head-over-heels roll. The woman moved the gun to follow his course, continuing to squeeze the trigger. Three more times. In the space of as many seconds, Bately took a bullet in his bloodied face, one in his left foot, and another in his back. He finished his roll at the feet of his killer and became as still as only a dead thing can be.

'It's done, Mu,' Aunt Matty rasped, lowering her arms, hands still wrapped around the butt of the gun.

'Two more, Barnaby,' Muriel gasped craning her neck to stare up at the sky.

But then her eyes closed and she fell forward.

'Muriel!' the older woman screamed, fearing the worst.

The worst happened as the half-breed eased upright, his tall, lean frame outlined on the brow of the hill. Muriel's torso slammed down along the length of the shotgun. The trigger was jolted and the firing pin hit the rear of the cartridge. The report was muffled by the woman's body. But it was loud enough to drive the tethered horses into a renewed bout of snorting panic. Muriel's chin hit the ground, immediately in line with the muzzle, as the charge belched from the confines of the barrel.

The entire front of Muriel Tree's head was ripped off and splashed in a gory swathe towards the base of the hill. All that was recognisable in the lumpy, slickly-wet stain on the dirt, was a tuft of golden hair.

'Muriel!' her sister-in-law screamed again, but in grief instead of warning now. She made to go to the side of the dead women, but halted and turned to stare at the approaching half-breed. Her expression was of abject defeat and misery. 'Why couldn't it have been me?' she implored helplessly, allowing the gun to drop from her hands.

Edge stepped across the broad line of slick blood stretching away from the shattered head of the dead woman. 'Because it was her, is all, ma'am,' he answered.

Anger quivered across her ugly face. 'And you don't give a damn, one way or the other?' she snarled as the tears spilled from her eyes.

Edge spat into the dirt. 'Makes no difference to me,' he admitted evenly.

'You disgust me!' the woman flung at him, using her sleeve to brush the tears from her deeply-lined cheeks.

'Long as one of you stays alive to claim the bull,' the half-breed amplified.

'Is money all you care about?'

'And staying alive. You want to start making the holes, ma'am?'

She spun around and strode angrily towards the wagon. 'Just three for Evans's skunks!' she growled. 'Mu'll get buried some place decent, where her grave can get took care of.'

Edge nodded.

The woman took both shovels from the wagon. 'Seein' as how you're so damn eager for the money, best you help me, mister. Longer the job takes, farther Evans'll take that bull away from us. You understand that?'

Edge let his Winchester fall to the ground and held out his hands. Aunt Matty tossed one of the shovels towards him. 'I dig,' he said.

# Chapter Eight

THE hours of darkness still had a long run ahead of them when Edge drove the wagon up out of the hollow. In front, his piebald gelding had replaced the dead stallion in the team. In the rear, the woman squatted beside Muriel Tree's dead body which lay wrapped in a blanket. She was giving her emotions free rein now and her sobs were loud in the night. Behind the rig as it rolled over the brow of the blood-stained hill, three identical mounds with three identical tombstones bore silent witness to the latest slaughter of the long trek from one border to another.

The half-breed's narrowed eyes scoured the country to the south-east whenever the wagon reached a vantage point. He was not looking for a sign of the two men with the bull for he guessed they were now far ahead. If they had not pulled out at the same time as Hollis Millard, Ray Irwin and Dale Bately, they would certainly have started running at the sound of the gun battle.

What he sought was a town, or a man-made trail that would indicate a town was within striking distance. For, irrespective of how he felt otherwise, he respected Mathilda Tree's wish to bury her sister-in-law in consecrated ground. But they had to reach a town fast, before the dead flesh of the woman began to putrefy. By morning would be best. Certainly as early as possible after the sun rose to quicken the decomposing process with its heat.

But the sun had been up an hour when he spotted the trail, cutting north to south towards a pass in the Gila Bend Mountains. To the north there was a broad panorama across low country with the horizon drawing closer as the heat shimmer thickened. In that direction, only the clearly defined trail showed that man had ever set foot on the land. He swung the wagon south, up into the mountains, and followed a trail that zigzagged to lessen the steepness of the climb. It took an hour to climb a couple of hundred feet and, when the team hauled the wagon up on to a broad shelf, Edge saw the tiny community. Half a mile away.

Hardly a town. A dozen or so crudely built shacks grouped together at the base of a rise which was pocked with tunnel entries. Closer to the shacks, and on level ground, was a much larger hole with a heap of recently dug earth at the side. Just as Edge got his first glimpse of the community, two men moved out from between the shacks. They carried a sack between them. The men were several yards short of the rim of the large hole when they saw the wagon rolling towards them.

They dropped the sack, drew their guns and fired. But the shots went straight up into the blueness of the morning sky, the revolvers held high above their heads.

'That shootin'?' Aunt Matty called from inside the wagon. Her voice had the tone of one who has just awakened. There was a scrabbling sound as she fought her way over the hay bales to get to the front of the wagon.

'Not *at* us,' Edge replied as a third man appeared. This time on the roof of one of the shacks. He waved frantically with a strip of yellow material.

Aunt Matty poked her head and shoulders through the front flaps of canvas and peered at the activity. All three men were shouting, but were too far off for their words to be more than unintelligible sounds. 'What is it?' she asked.

Edge slowed the team, but did not halt them. 'Mining camp,' he replied curtly.

'I guessed that!' the woman snapped. 'What's the shootin', shoutin' and flag-wavin' for?'

Edge halted the team now. The men with the guns holstered them and hefted the sack again. The flag-waver moved to the side of the shack roof and jumped down. 'Looks like they got bad sickness there. That's a quarantine flag, I figured.'

At the lip of the large hole, one of the men drew a knife and slit open the sack. White powder spilled from the split. Then both men hefted the sack again and hurled it into the centre of the hole. The powder billowed in a stark white cloud. It rose and then began to float down.

'You settle for a mass grave for your sister-in-law, ma'am?' Edge asked.

'That what it is?' she asked, shocked.

'They ain't just burying lime.'

The man with the yellow flag had advanced to a midway point between the shacks and the stationary wagon. He dropped the flag and cupped his hands around his mouth.

'You folks better stay clear of this place!' he bellowed. 'We hit stagnant water and fever's spread. Ten dead and as many dyin'.'

He and the two men at the side of the mass grave looked healthy enough. All were stripped to the waist and bulging with miner's muscles.

Edge hitched the reins around the brake lever and cupped his own hands to his lips. 'Two fellers with a stud bull pass by here?' he yelled.

'Middle of the night!' came the response. 'But steer clear of 'em, mister! We give 'em supplies and feed for the animals! Warned 'em it could have the sickness in it!'

'Which way they go?'

'Up through the pass to get on the Tucson Trail! You swing wide you want to go the same way!'

Edge glanced at Aunt Matty. 'Could be no one'll live through it, ma'am,' he pointed out. 'But if they do, I reckon the grave'll be well tended.'

The woman gave a curt nod. 'We don't bury her soon, could be we'll catch somethin' bad off her.'

The half-breed turned towards the mining camp again and cupped his hands as Aunt Matty struggled to the other side of the hay bales. 'We got us a dead woman!' he yelled. 'Obliged if you'd bury her.'

Even over such a distance, he saw the expressions of shocked suspicion that formed on the faces of the three miners. Then:

'Why the hell should we?' the spokesman demanded.

Edge was about to reply, when attention was switched from him to the rear of the wagon. He heard the tailgate drop, then the thud as Aunt Matty sprang to the ground. He leaned out of the seat to look along the side and saw the woman move off the trail, carrying the blanket-wrapped body as though it weighed no more than a couple of pounds.

'No farther, ma'am!' the man with the flag warned when she had closed to within a hundred yards of him.

Aunt Matty stopped abruptly, and knelt to rest the body reverently on the parched ground. From a pocket of her long coat she took some paper and a pencil. Still kneeling, she wrote a message. Then she took a pin from her hair to fix the paper to the blanket. She dropped the rest of the paper and the pencil and clasped her hands together in the attitude of prayer. The silence in the mountains took on the quality of that in a cathedral for the minute or so Mathilda Tree prayed.

'You will have my eternal thanks,' she called to the men as she got painfully to her feet.

She waited for a nod from each of them, then turned and started back towards the wagon. The men waited until she had climbed aboard, to sit beside Edge, before walking across to the body.

'You want to know what I wrote in the note?' she asked as Edge flicked the reins to start the team and tugged gently on them to steer the horses off the trail for a wide sweep around the shacks.

'Weren't addressed to me,' he replied.

'I said to put a marker on the grave for Muriel. I told them her full name. And I said to put: "Murdered by one of her husband's murderers". Not very holy like, but it tells the truth.'

The half-breed made no response.

'And, after I've got my share of the money, I'm comin' back here and I'm gonna see to it a proper monument is raised to that girl. What do you think of that, young feller?'

Aunt Matty sat very erect on the seat and folded her arms across her small breasts. A look of grim determination was carved on her face. Her eyes, drained of tears now, were as hard as dark pebbles as they stared up at the pass through which the trail snaked.

'I think you're a woman who most times does what she sets out to do, ma'am,' Edge replied softly.

She nodded her agreement and turned to fix him with the hard stare. 'Which proves I don't have to marry a man to learn somethin' from him.'

Wry humour curled back Edge's lips to show his teeth, gleaming among their surrounding of bristles. 'Hope that don't mean you've made five mistakes you'll regret the rest of your life,' he said.

But Mathilda Tree was not yet ready to try humour as a palliative for grief. And, as she stared ahead at the pass, there was no indication that she ever would. Muriel's death had hardened her: to a point, possibly, from which there could be no melting back to the gentler feminine characteristics.

'I'd thank you,' she said tautly, 'to treat my marriages the way you asked me to treat yours.'

The half-breed's expression became impassive. 'You're learning a lot, ma'am,' he told her softly as he veered the wagon back on to the trail. 'What's over is done. Don't do anybody any good messing with the past.'

'Unless a body's got to make others pay for messin' up the past.'

'I ain't about to argue with that,' he replied, and an easy silence settled between them.

Up at the pass, they were able to get a broad view across the country to the south and saw rock mountains dropping down to dirt foothills which, in turn, gave way to desert. They could pick out the trail, straight as an arrow's flight, angling south-east for Tucson, lost through the heat shimmer and over the horizon.

'Hungry for anything else except revenge?' Edge asked.

'How far to Texas?'

He halted the wagon. 'Two tombstones, I figure.'

Her mouthline grew firmer, and she rose from the seat. 'I guess your greed for the money matches mine for the lives those skunks. So if you reckon we got time to eat and rest, I'll go along with it.'

There was no more talk as, by tacit agreement, Edge attended to the needs of the horses while Aunt Matty set a fire and prepared a meal. Afterwards, the man shaved and then the woman used the still-hot water to wash the blood from the shotgun. She reloaded it and placed the gun behind the seat when the wagon started to roll again. The sun got hotter as it rose higher. The heat did not appear to diminish as the afternoon wore on. Dust kicked up by the hooves of the team billowed around Edge and Aunt Matty. They sucked it in through their mouths and nostrils and sweat pasted it to their faces.

A day, a night and half another day slid into a past which both had agreed was best forgotten. During that time they maintained a steady pace and discovered it was fast enough. For, from the anxious-to-talk, lonely men who tended the stage-line way stations, they learned that they were gradually over-hauling the two men with the high-priced bull. At first, the information they received indicated it was the bull which was holding up Evans and Jeb Stuart. Then, ten miles west of Tucson, they heard that Stuart had taken sick. The men had rested at the way station until, before dawn, Evans pulled out with the bull in tow. Stuart had awakened two hours later. He had been terrified rather than angry at being left behind. Despite his sickness, he had taken off at a gallop in pursuit of his boss.

'The fever?' Aunt Matty suggested as the wagon began to head along the final stretch of trail towards Tucson.

'Maybe.'

The woman looked as if she was about to spit, but transferred her disgust into words. 'And maybe he'll die before I get a chance to plug him, the lousy skunk.'

'What's the difference?'

'There ain't none for him. For me, all the difference in the world.'

Edge nodded. 'Guess so. But ain't no use getting into a sweat about it, ma'am.'

'Horses sweat, young feller,' she snapped. Men perspire. Ladies merely glow.'

Edge glanced at her. 'You're dazzling me,' he said wryly..

'I'll ask you to pay attention to your drivin', mister. And work the horses into a sweat. We can buy a new team in Tucson.'

'You paying?'

'Hock eveythin' I own if I have to. Why, Vic Evans could catch the fever same as Jeb Stuart.' The mere thought of being cheated in this way fed fresh fuel to the old woman's anger. She glowered at Edge. 'Well?' she demanded.

The half-breed cracked the reins over the backs of the horses. 'Hope for your sake Evans is,' he answered as the team broke into a gallop.

They were eight hours behind Evans at the last way station before Tucson: and six behind Stuart. When they reached town in the evening twilight they had pulled back two hours on the fat man. And Stuart was only thirty minutes behind his boss.

This information came from the man who ran the town livery where Mathilda Tree purchased a fresh team. It had been a good day for the man. Both Evans and Stuart had also done horse business with him. He was able to pass on the information that Jeb Stuart was real sick. Evans had looked fine.

After buying supplies to top up their diminished stock, Edge and the woman pulled out of Tucson under a night sky that was clouding over: the low-hung cover for the moon and stars being driven down from the north by a strengthening wind.

'That's Apache country you folks are headin' into!' the liveryman called after them.

Aunt Matty reached into the back of the wagon, took out the shotgun and rested it across her bony knees. Clear of the lights of the town, the grim lines of her expression altered slightly to depict a quiet apprehension as she surveyed the dark landscape.

'Seem to have heard somewhere that Injuns ain't supposed to

attack at night,' she said suddenly, her voice no louder than a whisper.

Edge nodded. 'Lot of white folks have heard that,' he answered, and spat down at the side of the trail. 'But a lot of Indians haven't.'

'Ain't anxious for myself,' she said after a long silence, during which she continued to peer around in every direction – even leaning to the side to stare behind the rolling wagon. 'Injuns are the same as the sickness, young feller. They could get Evans and Stuart before me.'

'Sure, ma'am,' Edge allowed. 'You already told me what the difference would be.'

'And think on, mister,' she rasped. 'Injuns get the animal, he'll be beef steaks soon as they get a fire lit.'

'Expensive food for thought,' he muttered.

The wind began to gust in more strongly from the north, sending the clouds racing across the sky and hurling dust high and hard at the team, wagon and the couple on the seat. Edge had to slow their progress, cracking his eyes to see the trail. If any sign had been left by their quarry, the wind blew it away or the dust covered it. But the trail was there to follow, swinging from south-east to due east as it headed for the weather-veiled Dragoon Mountains.

Some hours later the wind blew itself out and the dust settled but the clouds, although moving slowly, remained as thickly layered as during the storm. There were no stars to be seen and the moon showed as a pale, fuzzy disc. The clop of hooves and creak of the wagon timbers were the only constant sounds in the great silence. Sometimes, a coyote howled. Throughout the remainder of the night, Edge and Aunt Matty taking two hourly turns at driving while the other slept, they saw nobody – Apache or white man.

At dawn, the first light showed the trail cutting across a broad area of sand ridges, the land rising and dipping to no pattern. They stopped for thirty minutes to boil water for coffee and eat a cold breakfast. Then, two hours later, they saw a horse. Saddled, but with the reins hanging loose with no rider to hold them. The animal was foraging a mile ahead and several hundred yards to the south of the trail.

'Injuns don't ride with a saddle, do they?' Aunt Matty asked, straining her ancient eyes to peer at the distant horse through the billowing heat shimmer.

'It's like them fighting at night,' Edge answered. 'Some do. Some don't.'

The horse heard the sound of the wagon in the surrounding silence and froze and looked at the moving dark silhouette with the dust cloud rising behind it. Then, as if anxious not to lose his freedom from man, wheeled and broke into a gallop. The wagon rolled a further two miles before the couple up on the seat saw the man from whom the horse had escaped.

He lay on his back, sprawled at the side of a sand ridge just off the trail.

'It's Jeb Stuart!' Aunt Matty rasped in high excitement. She turned and reached into the wagon to snatch out the shotgun. The man was still more than a hundred yards away and the woman's exhilaration cooled as she surveyed him a second time. 'Hell, he looks dead!' she spat out.

'Looks is all,' the half-breed muttered. 'But he ain't.'

'How can you tell?'

'Ain't a buzzard in the sky, ma'am.'

Aunt Matty was non-plussed for a few moments. Then she swung the shotgun stock up to her shoulder and sighted along the barrel. She vented a low grunt. 'Skunk's tryin' to fool us. Aims to get the drop.'

'Maybe,' Edge allowed, holding the reins in just the one hand as he eased the Winchester out from the rear of the wagon to rest it across the seat. His hooded eyes stayed fixed on the man and, as the wagon rolled closer, he detected the steady rise and fall of Stuart's pudgy stomach. 'But I don't think so,' he added.

He hauled on the reins to bring the team to a stop, about fifty feet from the man lying sprawled on the ground. Then Stuart moved. His legs remained splayed and his arms stayed at his sides. It was just his hatless head that he raised so that he could peer pitifully along the trail at the stalled wagon.

'Help me?' he croaked. 'Please help me?'

His face was colourless behind the beads of sweat which

stood out from every pore, caught in the bristles of several days' growth of beard.

'We ain't here to help you, skunk!' the woman snarled, maintaining a steady aim at the target.

There was no indication that Jeb Stuart recognised Edge and Mathilda Tree. For long seconds he continued to stare at them. Then his neck muscles could support the weight of his head no longer and it smacked down into the sand. He spoke to the sky.

'I'm sick. Awful sick.' He moved again. But this time it was not voluntary. His entire frame spasmed with a fit of shivering. 'I'm cold. I'm dyin'.' His teeth chattered. 'Help me?'

Aunt Matty lowered the gun. 'Fever?' she asked Edge.

'I reckon.'

'The bastard!' the old woman snarled, and scrambled down from the seat. She sensed the cold blue eyes of the half-breed watching her and she glowered up at him. 'Don't you try to stop me, mister!' she warned.

Edge dug out the makings and began to roll a cigarette. 'He's going to die anyway,' he answered. 'You'll make it faster for him.'

'So we'll both be happier,' Aunt Matty retorted, and strode towards the helpless man.

Edge lit his cigarette and sucked the smoke deep into his lungs. The woman halted beside the sick Jeb Stuart. Stuart raised his head again, squinting against the sun. For a moment, the pain went out of his pallid face to be replaced by terror.

'Mathilda Tree!' he gasped.

'That's me, Jeb Stuart.' Her voice was lifeless, the words spat out like they were pieces of something that tasted putrid. 'You got any last thing to say?'

The terror was swept from the slickly moist features. 'Yes, Miss Tree. That Mr Evans, he run out on me. Just 'cause I was sick and couldn't keep up. I want for you to kill him. I know you won't be doin' it for me. But I want for you to do it.'

From his seat on the wagon, Edge saw the hatred expand on the woman's ugly face. 'Kinda puts you in a spot, don't it, ma'am?' he called.

Stuart's head fell back into the sand. Aunt Matty leaned forward, to rest the shotgun muzzle under the submissive jaw. She squeezed the trigger. The man's head disintegrated into soggy crimson-stained chunks which spewed across the hot sand. Buzzards appeared from out of the heat shimmer and soared on the thermals.

'Favours don't do a dead man no good, mister!' the woman called sourly, staring down coldly at the decapitated corpse as the sound of the gunshot diminished across the wilderness.

Edge climbed down from the wagon and went to the rear. He lowered the tail-gate and hauled out two bales of hay.

'We fed the horses this mornin',' the woman growled, turning away from the body.

'Burn him before you bury him,' the half-breed instructed evenly. 'On account of the fever. And don't touch him.'

'Nice you're concerned about me,' Aunt Matty answered with heavy sarcasm.

Edge sat down at the shaded side of the wagon, leaning his back against a wheel. 'Me I'm concerned about,' he told the woman. 'I got to ride with you.'

'My mistake,' Aunt Matty snarled, flinging down the shotgun and returning to the wagon to get the bales.

She broke them open and built a pyre around the dead man. Edge tossed her a match and she lit the tinder-dry hay. Flames leapt high, then grey smoke curled higher. The buzzards kept their distance. The fire died around the corpse and left it as a blackened cinder. The fine sand would not allow a deep hole to be dug. The woman used the shotgun to tip Jeb Stuart's remains into the shallow grave, and buried the weapon with him beneath the sand. The inevitable marble tombstone was set in place at the head of the mound.

'It irks me he died happy,' she said with weary ill-temper as she dragged her feet back to the wagon. 'I should have stood off so he didn't see me. And watched him die slow of the fever.'

Edge eased upright from his seat by the wheel, brushing sand from his pants. 'I feel for you, lady,' he muttered as he climbed on to the wagon seat.

'You can always back out on this deal!' she snapped in retort to his tone. 'I don't need you no more, mister!' she sniffed as she flopped down on to the seat. 'It's just me and Evans now. One against one.'

'Figure I'll stay,' the half-breed said, unhitching the reins and flicking them. 'With the odds even and you so well practised, I reckon Evans don't stand a chance.'

'You bet he don't!' Aunt Matty growled.

'I did, ma'am. Twenty-five grand.'

# Chapter Nine

THE smoke which had driven off the buzzards attracted the Apaches. Not many of them; a hunting party of about a dozen. Edge had been aware of them for a long time, riding about three miles to the south on a parallel course with the wagon. But the woman, withdrawn into a world of private contemplation, did not spot the Indians for at least an hour after they first showed through the shimmer of heat.

'Injuns!' she exclaimed, reaching for the shotgun that was no longer there. The absence of the gun sharpened her fear and she stared at the half-breed's hard-set profile. 'What we gonna do?'

'You could try praying,' Edge advised sourly. 'But I reckon your stock's sunk pretty low in heaven.'

'Talk sense!' she snarled.

Her tone didn't provoke him to anger. He glanced at the distant Indians, then back at the trail. 'Ain't much to do, ma'am. Short of not bothering them. Then maybe they won't bother us.'

'But they're trailin' us!'

'Maybe only means that what they're after headed the same way we are.'

'What if they're after us?' Aunt Matty insisted.

Edge spat. 'Worrying about Apaches never been known to scare them off.'

The woman either accepted the half-breed's point or decided there was nothing to be gained by further discussion. She lapsed into silence and maintained a constant surveillance on the Indians. The sun dipped low behind them and the Apaches could be seen more clearly as the heat haze retreated. Then the darkness crept in over the land and the Indians were lost to sight. Aunt Matty began to shoot frightened glances in every direction, her head cocked on one side, ears straining to pick up a sound of stealthy approach.

When full night fell, Edge called a halt in the foothills under the western slopes of the Dragoons. He drove the wagon into a gully with a dead-end at a cliff face four hundred feet away. The cliff and the sides of the gully were about fifty feet high.

'They can trap us in here, damn it!' Aunt Matty growled after a rapid survey when Edge stopped the wagon.

'Sure can if we stay,' he agreed, leaping down from the seat.

'Then you reckon it is us they're after?'

'They been trailing something,' he answered as he unhitched the team. 'And I ain't seen nothing but them and us all afternoon. Be obliged if you'd pitch the tent and set a fire.'

If the old woman's rheumatics were bothering her, she showed no sign of it as she complied with Edge's request. She took her lead from him and worked fast. He told her where to set up the tent and build the fire. Then he broke open all but one of the hay bales and spread the feed across the rocky floor of the gully. The tethered horses began to eat. Then, Edge carrying the remaining bale, and Aunt Matty his Winchester and her newly acquired Tranter, they went back down the gully to where the sides became less sheer. They climbed and it was not until they reached the top that the woman began to pant from the exertion and grunt with the pain. They crawled along the gully rim, back to the point where they could look down upon the firelit scene of the camp.

Aunt Matty sprawled out on her back and took several minutes to recover. Then she rolled over on to her belly, like Edge, and peered downwards.

'What if they don't come?' she whispered.

'Then it's going to be a long, cold night,' Edge muttered in reply. 'No more restful than if we were down there.'

The woman nodded. 'Guess so, young feller.'

It was a long, stiff-limbed hour later when they saw the first of the Apaches. Aunt Matty caught her breath and reached to claw a hand around Edge's upper arm. The half-breed pulled his arm away from the grasp and took a match from his shirt pocket. A second Indian had appeared beside the first and the two moved silently forward towards the campsite at the dead end of the gully. Both were dressed in buck-skin shirts and leggings and wore headbands, but no feathers and were carrying primed bows. They advanced in utter silence towards the fringe glow of the diminishing fire, heads swinging slowly from left to right as their dark eyes raked the camp. The four horses, their fill eaten, watched the advance of the intruders with the same intensity as Edge and the woman.

Then the Apaches halted, stared at the tent, looked at each other, nodded, and drew their bowstrings. As they released the arrows, their mouths gaped wide to vent howls of triumph. The sounds of the shafts ripping through the tent canvas and thudding into the ground beneath was drowned by whoops from many more than two throats.

The rest of the Apache band sprinted into view as the two scouts lunged forward snatching fresh arrows from their pouches to fit to the bows. The other ten braves wielded a mixture of weapons – bows, knives, tomahawks and revolvers. Their raddled faces all wore matching expressions of greed.

Edge struck the match on a rock, dragged the hay bale to the rim of the gully and set light to it. He closed his eyes to keep from being dazzled by the sudden flare, and used the Winchester's muzzle to tip the bale over. Then he opened his eyes and canted the rifle downwards, moving himself forward with his elbows.

'Killing time again, lady!' he snapped, pumping the repeater action and squeezing off his first shot.

Some of the Apaches had halted abruptly and curtailed their excitement before the flaming bale started to tumble. For they had become suspiciously aware of the hay scattered under their moccasined feet. It was at these braves that Edge aimed first, sighting down the barrel at their upturned faces as the Apaches stared in horror at the falling ball of fire. Two took bullets in the face and a third was hit in the back of the head as he whirled round.

The nine surviving braves became aware of the danger. Four turned to lunge back the way they had come. Five more sought the cover of the wagon.

'The runaways!' Edge yelled.

The flaming hay bale crashed to the gully floor and the impact exploded flares in all directions. The scattered hay caught light and a dozen small fires sprang up and spread.

Aunt Matty responded to Edge's shout. With the revolver held in her two-handed grip, she matched him shot for shot at the running Indians. They only had to bring down three. The fourth had been showered by raining flames and writhed in his agony as a human torch – clothes and hair burning fiercely. The other three sprawled to the ground, flesh pumping crimson from bullet wounds.

The braves under the wagon reacted to the advancing sea of fire at the same time as the horses. The animals, purposely tethered loosely, reared free and bolted. Snorting in terror and pain, they lunged for the dead end of the gulley. Maddened by panic, they reared again, trying the impossible – to climb the sheer wall of rock.

As the Apaches under the wagon broke out and ran towards the flames, they had no time to retaliate against the defenders turned attackers. Edge ignored them, swinging his Winchester towards the helpless team. The three remaining shells in the rifle dropped three of the horses. Then he drew his Colt and had to fire three bullets into the last horse before the animal dropped dead.

No more shots were fired, by Edge or the woman. Below, at ground level, the terrified braves could see just one dimension of fire. From above, the watchers were able to see just how wide the moving line of flames was. And they had a horrifying view of five men plunging into the flames. They were not able to see them drop. But, as the wall of fire moved on, ravenous for fresh fuel, they did see the charred bodies left in its wake.

Horrifying, but neither Edge nor Mathilda Tree experienced horror at what they saw. Both were too familiar with death. And both had a vivid recollection of the arrows thudding into the tent.

Aunt Matty sighed as she rose painfully to her feet. 'Take back what I said awhile ago, young feller,' she croaked as black smoke from the fire billowed around them. 'Reckon I need you even more than you need me. I ain't much, but I figure I'm worth more than twenty-five thousand dollars to me.'

Edge ejected the final spent shell from the Winchester and started to reload. 'No extra charge, ma'am,' he told her. 'Twenty-five is still all you're worth to me.'

She became rigid at the taunt, but kept her temper under control. And she watched in tight-lipped silence as he finished reloading the rifle and then did the same with the chambers of the Colt. Then:

'What now, mister? Injuns didn't get us, but got most everythin' that was ours.'

'We find where they left their ponies,' Edge answered as he stood up.

'You find where they left their ponies,' Aunt Matty countered, and looked down through the smoke into the gully. 'I've got to get somethin' soon as the fire's out.'

He didn't have to ask what it was and he responded with a curt nod and started back along the gully rim and then down the incline. The woman followed him and, on the gully floor, stood watching the dying fire as Edge went in search of the dead braves' horses. He had found them and cut out the two strongest-looking mounts when the woman emerged from the blind gully, struggling under the weight of the marble tombstone. She had taken the time to clean off the soot, so that the black lettering stood out against the stone.

'Wouldn't be right Vic Evans didn't get treated the same as the rest of his murderin' skunks!' she challenged.

Edge held open a rawhide saddle-bag and the woman eased the grave marker into it. 'Your party, ma'am,' he rasped sourly. 'I'm with you as long as you keep doing the treating.'

# Chapter Ten

THE Woodrow Ryan spread was north-east of El Paso in a broad, verdant valley watered by a shallow river that flowed westwards to join the Rio Grande. There was a town sited on the northern slope of the valley at the eastern end and it was to here that Edge and Aunt Matty were directed from El Paso. They were no longer riding Apache ponies. Instead, strong stallions the woman had bought in Deming, New Mexico territory. It was in the early morning that they reached the border town and learned they were all the hours of darkness behind Vic Evans and the bull.

Two hours outside El Paso, they rode past a boundary marker which told them they were on Ryan land. They swung eastwards into the valley and it took them a further three hours of hard riding to reach Greenville. It was a town that was well named, for it overlooked a vast acreage of fine grazing and woodland. On the way, they had past no more markers to show they had moved off Ryan property. They had seen a lot of beef on the hoof, but no people.

In Greenville there were people, most of whom went about their daily business without casting a second glance at the weary looking, dust-covered couple who rode through town. And neither Edge nor Aunt Matty paid any attention to anything about Greenville except a wagon that was parked outside the Lone Star Saloon. The wagon had high sides and a conventional tail-gate, but with a framework of wooden bars fixed on the top of it. The doleful eyes of the white bull peered disinterestedly out through the bars.

Two broadly built men were lounging in rocking chairs at either side of the hotel entrance. And these were the only people in the spick and span town who kept the approaching riders under close scrutiny. They continued to watch with unblinking eyes as Edge and Aunt Matty slid from their saddles and hitched their horses to the rail.

'Ryan bought that there bull yet?' Aunt Matty demanded, jerking a thumb towards the wagon then starting to unfasten the bulky saddle-bag holding the last tombstone.

Both men got grim looks on their faces and used the forward rock of their chairs to help them upright.

'*Mr* Ryan's business is his own, lady,' the one on the left snapped.

'Work for him?' Edge asked evenly, sliding the Winchester from the saddle-boot and canting it up to his shoulder.

'Two of his top hands,' the one on the right drawled. 'What's it to you?'

Edge pursed his lips. 'Nothing, unless you happen to know whether he's still paying fifty grand for the beef.'

Aunt Matty, working with sweaty faced determination, had managed to ease the heavy grave marker out of the saddle-bag. She had to hold it low down, in both hands. The two men on the hotel stoop stared at the tombstone with dumbstruck awe. The woman grinned at them. She had done a lot of grinning, smirking and quiet smiling over the final, untroubled leg of the long journey.

The taller man was the first to recover from the surprise. 'I told the lady – Mr Ryan's business is – '

'Ours when he's doing it with us,' Edge cut in, and started up the step to the sidewalk.

Both men went for their guns, hands moving as if at the dictate of some linking machine. Edge whirled and slapped down the Winchester, pumping the action. Before the revolvers were clear of the holsters, the rifle was aimed at the head of the bull.

'Drop the irons, fellers,' the half-breed said evenly. 'Or Ryan's in on the dead meat business.'

'What is this?' the shorter man demanded.

Aunt Matty sniffed. 'Drop the guns like the man says and you can come and find out,' she invited flatly.

'Mr Ryan!'

It was the shorter one again, his voice raised to a bellow. Edge's narrowed eyes swept over the men, who were frozen in the act of drawing their guns, barrels not yet clear of the holsters. Then to Aunt Matty who continued to express confidence, her slender frame not bending under the weight of the last tombstone. Finally, along the street. The citizenry of Greenville displayed total indifference to what was happening in front of the Lone Star Hotel.

A window banged open on the second floor of the hotel. Both Edge and Aunt Matty glanced up. The bull remained firmly under threat of death and the tombstone stayed solidly held. Framed in the upstairs window was a man of middle-years. Big-built and well-dressed. Wearing a neatly trimmed grey beard.

'Guess you're Mathilda Tree and the hired gun,' he called down evenly.

'Oh, my God!' a recognisable voice croaked from within the room. There was a sudden splashing of water.

Woodrow Ryan snapped his head round to look at Vic Evans. 'Stay where you are!' he ordered. Then he looked down into the street again. 'Apaches didn't get you over Arizona way, uh?' he asked reflectively. Then he gave a curt nod. 'Since you made it I reckon you deserve a hearing. Come on up.'

'No!' Evans shrieked, with another splash of water. 'They'll kill me!'

Ryan sighed. 'Quit whinning, Evans!' he growled without turning this time. Then he got frost into his dark-eyed gaze as he stared down at Aunt Matty and Edge. 'No one kills nobody on Ryan land unless Woodrow Ryan says so.' He moderated his tone. 'Let 'em up, fellers.'

He stepped back out of sight and the window banged closed.

'Okay,' the taller man allowed. 'But we keep our damn guns.'

'Edge?' Aunt Matty asked. 'You don't want to kill that bull.'

The half-breed pursed his lips. 'Back in the holsters – all the way.'

'You mean any harm to Mr Ryan?' the shorter one wanted to know.

'Treat folks the way they treat me.'

There were the sounds of the guns being returned to the holsters. Edge slanted the rifle to his shoulder again. It was still cocked.

'The lady first,' one of Ryan's men said, in the tone of an order.

Aunt Matty nodded and went through the open double doorway into the shady interior of the hotel lobby. It was a lot cooler in there, the air fresh with the scent of scrubbed timber. The two men held back only a moment, realised they could make no more demands, and followed the woman. The bespectacled desk clerk pretended the same disinterest as the people out on the street and was suddenly very busy with paperwork as the group crossed to the foot of the stairway and started up.

'Vic Evans's room?' Aunt Matty called.

The clerk swallowed hard. 'Five.'

'Thanks.'

'But you didn't ought to go in, lady. He's taking a bath.'

Aunt Matty sniffed. 'He came into the world naked,' she said with soft-voiced menace.

The clerk gulped again.

At the head of the stairs, the woman strode purposefully towards the appropriately numbered door. It was closed. Ryan's men kept shooting anxious glances over their shoulders at the impassive Edge. The half-breed showed no expression, his lips pursed as if he was on the point of whistling a melancholy tune.

'Come on in,' Ryan yelled as he heard the footfalls out on the landing.

'Open the door for a burdened lady, young feller,' Aunt Matty said to the taller of Ryan's men.

'I ain't gonna take – '

Edge snapped the rifle down to level it. 'Cheaper to blast you than the bull,' he warned softly.

Both men became like statues again. Then the tall one inched forward. 'It'll be me comin' in first, Mr Ryan,' he called, much louder than necessary.

The rancher ventured a short laugh. 'After what I've heard, understand why you're nervous, ma'am,' he said. 'Come on in, Harding.'

The handle rattled and Harding pushed the door open. Aunt Matty had stepped to the side. Now she leaned forward to peer between the frame and the solidly built body of Harding. She showed the broadest grin of all. There was the sound of a man catching his breath. It had to be Evans. Harding moved into the room, and Aunt Matty shuffled in behind him, only now beginning to show the strain of hauling the heavy tombstone.

'You sure look like you're seein' a ghost, Vic,' the woman taunted. 'But I sure enough ain't one.'

The second Ryan man did not need a jab in the back from the Winchester to urge him into the room. He wasn't about to miss the action. Edge moved through the doorway only a moment behind him.

'Mr Ryan!' Evans pleaded. 'She's even got a tombstone for me!'

The terrified man sat quivering and naked in a tin bathtub. His clean, white skin contrasted starkly with the black scum coating the water to hide him from the waist down.

Ryan ignored Evans. He was seated on a rattan chair at the side of the bed. 'Something you people should know,' he said evenly, 'before there's more killin' on account of the animal.' He started to rise. 'There was a mistake and – '

'He's the mistake!' Aunt Matty cut in, continuing to stare fixedly at the handsome face of the man in the tub. 'He was born a mistake and he's been makin' 'em ever since.'

'Mathilda, listen to Mr Ryan!' Evans pleaded. 'The bull ain't – '

'Important!' the woman snarled.

Footfalls sounded on the stairway, clearly heard through the open doorway.

'You've been a snivellin' cowardly skunk all your life, Vic!' Aunt Matty snarled. 'Can't expect you to die any other way, I'm thinkin'.'

The newcomer was on the landing now, quickening his pace towards room five. There was a frenetic disturbance under the scummed water. Aunt Matty gave a shriek of horror as she saw a look of cunning replace the fear on Evans's face. Then his hands came clear of the bath water. He used the same double grip Aunt Matty favoured. It was a Colt .44 he aimed at her. As the woman released the tombstone and a small man wearing a green eyeshade pulled up short in the doorway, Harding and his sidekick went for their guns again.

'One mistake's enough!' Edge warned.

'Leave it!' Ryan bellowed above the crash of the chunk of marble against the floor.

The man in the doorway ducked from sight. Aunt Matty fumbled in the pocket of her long coat. Evans squeezed the trigger of the Colt. He hadn't cocked it. He gave a hoarse cry of horror as the trigger remained inert. Then his wet thumb slipped off the dripping hammer as Aunt Matty levelled her gun. The double-action needed no cocking. The Tranter exploded in the two-handed grip. The woman rocked back only slightly with the recoil. The Colt fired an instant later, as Evans opened his mouth to scream. But he was dead before he could utter a sound. It was Aunt Matty who added noise to the moment of silence following the gunfire. She gave a grunt of sadness as she looked down at her own blood.

The range was just a few feet and both were freak shots. The woman's bullet plunged into Evans's chest, burrowed a hole through his heart and drove out of his back without touching a bone. It punched a hole in the bath and the dirty water began to drain out and spread across the bare floorboards. The dead man's bullet angled downwards, hit the marble tombstone and ricochetted on to a new course. It penetrated Aunt Matty's lower stomach and didn't stop until it had smashed through her entrails to puncture a lung. She sat down hard and fell backwards, to lean against the door-jamb. Blood bubbled in her throat, but she continued to live.

'Reckon that settles it,' Woodrow Ryan said with a nod, voice and expression totally lacking emotion. 'No way of knowin' which party really owned the beef. So I give Mr Evans the same chance I figured the lady had. Can't pay a dead man.'

He reached into the inside pocket of his well cut jacket and drew out an envelope.

'Safe to come in now, Mr Ryan?' the little man with the eye-shade called.

'Sure, Herbie,' the rancher answered.

The man stepped nervously into the doorway and looked with shocked eyes from the man in the emptying tub to the raggedly breathing woman.

'Read what my telegraph said, Herbie,' Ryan instructed, as he drew the flap out of the envelope.

Edge saw the money. All hundred dollar bills. Not nearly enough to add up to fifty thousand. Then his hooded-eyed gaze raked across the room to fix upon the little man.

'Lady oughta have a doctor, Mr Ryan,' the man whined.

A doctor wouldn't be able to help Aunt Matty. Her ugly face was bloodless. The dark stain on the front of her coat, enlarging by the moment, showed where most of her blood was going.

'Read, Herbie,' Ryan insisted impatiently.

Herbie unfolded an old-looking telegraph form. He glanced around at everybody, then cleared his throat. 'Addressed to Barnaby Tree. At a town way up north. Signed by Mr Ryan. Reads like this: "Bull all is claimed to be, will pay five thousand dollars for the animal." That's all.' He blinked as he made another survey of the room.

'Beat it, Herbie,' Ryan ordered.

The little man disappeared from the doorway, happy to leave. He began to run after taking his first few steps.

'That was the mistake,' the rancher said. 'Somewhere along the line, that five thousand got another zero added to it. I ain't fool enough to offer no fifty grand for an animal that ain't proved itself at stud.' His dark eyes moved from the dying Aunt Matty, to Edge, and back again. 'Hope you folks will take my word for that.'

Edge nodded. 'Fifty grand was always too much.'

'Young feller,' Aunt Matty said weakly, forcing the words around the rising blood. 'You divide it up the way we agreed.'

Her eyes, becoming glazed as death encroached, remained fixed upon the body in the bath as the water, its black scum now streaked with red, widened its staining of the scrubbed floor.

Ryan handed the money to the half-breed, who counted off twenty-five of the bills and folded them into his pocket.

'I'm gonna die, Edge,' the woman said, and a trickle of blood spilled from the corner of her mouth and laid a trail down to the hair-sprouting mole. 'That two and a half thousand that's mine . . . you fix for me to be taken back and buried along with Mu?'

The half-breed gave the woman's half of the money back to Ryan. 'You know the local mortician better than me, feller,' he said. 'Fix it. She'll need a marker. I'll tell him where.'

Woodrow Ryan seemed on the point of expressing his resentment at the half-breed's demanding attitude. But he met the cold stare of the ice blue eyes. 'I'll have my men take care of it,' he promised as Edge turned towards the door.

'Do that.'

'He was the worst of the lot,' Aunt Matty rasped, the words powering more blood from both corners of her mouth now.

Edge halted and looked back as he was about to step over the frail dying form. All the water had drained from the bathtub now, to expose Evans in complete, lilywhite nakedness.

'The skunk with the biggest stink,' the woman went on. 'His whole life was nothing but a filthy, rotten, stinking . . . ' Her beautiful body folded forward to hide her ugly face and Mathilda Tree died.

Edge clicked his tongue against the roof of his mouth as he moved out into the hallway. 'Yeah,' he muttered. 'But nobody can say he didn't die clean.'